"I'm still very curious, you know," Justin said.

He levered his long body away from the door. "Maybe you're not the little snob you appeared to be last night." He stopped when he was even with her and looked down into her eyes, his own dark with mysterious energy. "You told me very flatly that you were bored by my company."

The charge of boredom rankled Liz. "I'm sorry." She almost smiled. Justin Hogan would arouse a lot of emotions, but boredom would certainly not be one of them. She wouldn't tell him that, though; he was too sure of himself. Let him wonder.

Then, suddenly, he touched her cheek, lightly, briefly, with just the tips of his fingers. The effect was electrifying. All her satisfaction dissipated.

He spoke in a low, sexy voice that sent chills through her. "Maybe I can change your mind."

Dear Reader,

Welcome to Silhouette Romance—experience the magic of the wonderful world where two people fall in love. Meet heroines who will make you cheer for their happiness, and heroes (be they the boys next door or handsome, mysterious strangers) who will win your heart. Silhouette Romances reflect the magic of love—sweeping you away with books that will make you laugh and cry, heartwarming, poignant stories that will move you time and time again.

In the next few months, we're publishing romances by many of your all-time favorite authors such as Diana Palmer, Brittany Young, Annette Broadrick and many others. Your response to these and other authors in Silhouette Romance has served as a touchstone for us, and we're pleased to bring you more books with Silhouette's distinctive medley of charm, wit and—above all—*romance*.

During 1991, we have many special events planned. Don't miss our WRITTEN IN THE STARS series. Each month in 1991, we're proud to present readers with a book that focuses on the hero—and his astrological sign.

I hope you'll enjoy this book and all of the stories to come. Come home to romance—Silhouette Romance—for always!

Sincerely,

Tara Gavin
Senior Editor

MARION SMITH COLLINS

Home
To Stay

Silhouette *Romance*

Published by Silhouette Books New York

America's Publisher of Contemporary Romance

SILHOUETTE BOOKS
300 E. 42nd St., New York, N.Y. 10017

HOME TO STAY

ISBN: 0-373-08773-X

First Silhouette Books printing February 1991

Printed in the U.S.A.

Books by Marion Smith Collins

Silhouette Intimate Moments

Another Chance #179
Better Than Ever #252
Catch of the Day #320

Silhouette Romance

Home To Stay #773

MARION SMITH COLLINS

has written non-fiction for years, but only recently has she tried her hand at novels. She is already the author of several contemporary romances and has no plans to stop.

She's a devoted traveler and has been to places as far-flung as Rome and Tahiti. Her favorite country for exploring, however, is the United States because, she says, it has everything.

In addition, this mother of two children has been a public relations director. Her love of art inspired her to run a combination gallery and restaurant for several years.

She lives with her husband of thirty years in Georgia.

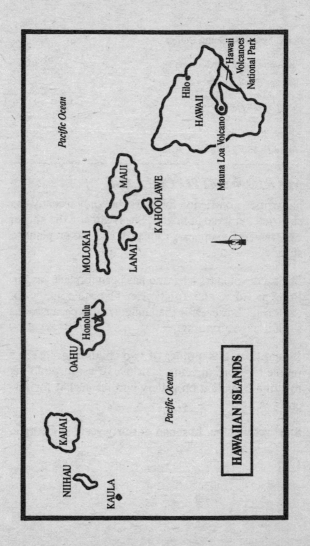

Pacific Ocean

Hawaii Volcanoes National Park

Hilo

HAWAII

Mauna Loa Volcano

MAUI

KAHOOLAWE

MOLOKAI

LANAI

OAHU

Honolulu

KAUAI

NIIHAU

KAULA

Pacific Ocean

HAWAIIAN ISLANDS

Prologue

The bright sun over paradise looked down on Elizabeth Ennis as she tried to find a parking place among all the cars in front of the commanding officer's quarters at Barber's Point, Naval Air Station on Oahu. At last.

She got out of the car and made her way along the neatly raked walk on shaky legs. She stepped into the foyer, closed the door behind her and leaned against it in overwhelming relief. Only then did she become aware of voices, clinking glassware and the laughter coming from the living room. A party, she thought, her heart sinking another notch. She should have known—all those cars—but her brain wasn't working too well this afternoon.

Her mother's head appeared around the corner. "Liz, darling, you're home early. Taylor isn't with you? Well, never mind. Come and say hello to our guests."

"Mother, I . . ." But her mother had disappeared.

Liz covered her mouth with her hand and closed her burning eyes for a minute. She should be used to this household by now, having been brought up in a family where socializing often crowded out personal emergencies.

But this time it was hard, so hard. A quick appearance, she told herself, then she could escape. She breathed deeply to bring some kind of control to her shaking limbs, levered herself away from the support of the door and turned to check her appearance in the ormolu mirror.

Lord, she looked like death warmed over. Her blue-green eyes were sunken and dark, her skin and lips colorless. She couldn't go in looking like this. Quickly she fumbled in the heavy case slung over her shoulder for a lipstick, searching among filters and rolls of film. Liz never carried a purse; money and passport and other essentials were packed in her camera case. It was the one thing she was never without.

A few minutes later Liz entered the living room. She tried to ignore the pounding in her ears as she spoke politely to several people. She knew the routine. Her body was unnaturally rigid and every step she took was an effort, but she kept her head high and a smile on her face. The smile didn't reach her eyes, however, and the sincerity was forced. Only she knew how forced.

Groups formed and reformed as she moved through the crowd like a pro, speaking to people she knew, introducing herself to the others who stopped her, curious about the admiral's daughter. All the time her eyes were scanning the crowd, seeking her father. When she spied him, she changed direction, heading across the room like a radar beam homing in on its target.

Rear Admiral Robert T. Ennis, USN, was the center of a group that included a commander, two captains, one woman—Fran Mason of the Hawaii Visitors' Bureau—and another man, a stranger to Liz. The stranger was distinguished in this gathering by the fact that he was one of the few men present dressed in civilian clothes.

Daddy, she cried silently, but her father hadn't spotted her.

Instead the tall man at her father's side raised his head. His gaze narrowed on Liz for a moment and skimmed down her body in automatic appraisal, taking in every curve before returning to her face. The experience wasn't unusual but it was especially distasteful today, right now.

Suddenly his eyes locked with hers, checking her progress as effortlessly as if he'd ordered her to halt. The mask that was her protective veneer threatened to crack under the force of the man's piercing green gaze.

Liberation came in the form of a steward at her elbow offering a tray of drinks. Shaking her head at the man, she resumed her journey. Fran Mason would have been a help, but the older woman had moved on, as had the others in the group. If she could just get to her father, if the stranger would leave them alone for a minute...

The admiral realized that he no longer had his companion's full attention. He followed the direction of the man's gaze. When he saw his daughter, he smiled. "Liz, honey, come here," he said, holding out his arm.

Liz went gratefully into his supportive embrace. She was vaguely aware of the stranger's taking her measure from a great height.

Her father said, "Liz, I'd like for you to meet Justin Hogan."

"Miss Ennis." His left hand was in his pocket and his right held a drink, so he acknowledged the introduction with a slight inclination of his head. Up close, his expression was no less unrelenting, but unreadable.

The pounding in her ears increased, and she missed the rest of her father's statement. "How do you do?" she said mechanically. "Daddy, I..."

But her father was responding to a genial summons from her mother on the other side of the room. "Excuse me," he said. "Liz, take care of Justin." He removed the blessed support of his arm.

Turning to Justin Hogan, Liz sighed. Then suddenly she was wincing from the scowl that had furrowed his brow. The animosity radiating from the man was almost tangible. Why? she wondered, confused.

"I understand good wishes are in order."

Liz looked at him blankly. He took her left hand in his and indicated the large diamond there.

Liz jerked her hand away as though she had touched a hot stove. Pain stabbed anew at various places in her body—her stomach, her head, her heart. She twisted nervously at the ring and tried to come up with a conventional answer, something orthodox and proper.

But this last reminder was too much. She felt the blood drain from her face, her palms were suddenly damp, her head began to swim. Oh, good Lord, help! She was going to faint right here. Her eyes sought those of Justin Hogan in mute appeal.

Without fuss, he responded. His strong arm encircled her waist and he guided her unobtrusively toward the patio doors. When they were outside he put her into a chair and pushed her head down to her knees. "Breathe deeply," he commanded. He kept his large hand on her head, presumably to be sure she followed orders.

Liz drank in great gulps of air, and soon her swimming senses began to quiet. "Thank you," she said, raising her head slowly, testing her control in stages. She was steadier than she'd been seconds ago, but still shaky. She rested her head against the back of the chair and closed her eyes. If she could just stay here for a few minutes, without talking, without thinking...

"Are you pregnant?" Justin Hogan asked harshly.

Her eyes flew open, but the frozen expression on her face remained. "No," she answered evenly.

He stood glaring at her. His jacket was open. He thrust both hands into the pockets of his dark slacks, stretching them tightly over his flat stomach and muscular thighs. A lightweight blazer sat easily across his broad shoulders. As she'd noticed earlier, he was an extremely tall man, probably six-three or -four.

As they held her gaze, his green eyes altered color, became shadowy and inscrutable. He raked a hand through his thick, dark hair and swung away from her. "That was a rude question and none of my business."

"Yes," Liz agreed. She noticed that he didn't apologize for it. Shrugging off her lassitude, she gripped the arms of the chair and pushed herself to her feet. This man, a guest of her parents, had rescued her from an embarrassing collapse. She owed him the courtesy of a thank-you. "I appreciate you getting me out of there before I embarrassed everyone by fainting."

He shrugged lightly, as though her gratitude made him uncomfortable, and moved to the edge of the lanai, where he half turned toward the garden.

Her father often entertained vacationing dignitaries. Something about this man shouted VIP. She should make an effort.... "Are you visiting the islands for the first time, Mr. Hogan?"

He glanced over his shoulder. "You don't listen very well, do you, Miss Ennis?" he asked in a deceptively mild voice. "Your father explained that I live on the island of Hawaii."

"I'm sorry."

"Sorry?" He swung to face her. "Forgive me for doubting your sincerity, Miss Ennis, but ever since you entered that room with your very attractive nose in the air, you've made it clear you were bored by your father's guests."

Bored? Where did he get that impression? Then, finally, Liz dropped her chin, letting her hair sweep forward to hide the bleakness in her expression. She stared at her hands. Without thought, she twisted the ring off and gripped it until it bit into the skin of her palm. The physical pain relieved some of her emotional shock and gave her the shot of defiance she needed to get herself out of here.

Let the man believe she was bored. She didn't really care, and it was better than the humiliating truth. She raised her head, meeting his gaze full on, and smiled.

"You're right, Mr. Hogan. I'm bored stiff. So, if you will please excuse me . . . ?"

Chapter One

A lean, spry woman in her sixties opened the front door. "You must be Miss Ennis," she said. "Come in. Come in. I'm Annie, the Hogans' housekeeper."

Liz crossed the threshold into a spacious open-air entryway, tiled in sienna squares and lighted softly from a hidden source against the impending promise of twilight. "Thank you. Yes, I'm Elizabeth Ennis." From her height of five-nine, she had to look down at the woman. "I'm very sorry to be late," she added.

"Mrs. Hogan is waiting for you in her morning room, if you'll please follow me. She has been terribly worried," Annie continued with a sideways glance, which, despite its brevity, took in every detail of Liz's disheveled appearance.

Liz smiled and followed the housekeeper down a long hallway. Her bulky camera case bumped against her thigh as she walked.

Annie paused at an open door and gestured for Liz to enter. Liz smoothed her hair; her pumpkin-colored skirt and jacket were beyond help, streaked with dirt, and her pumps looked as though she'd run a marathon in them. "Thank you, Annie," she said.

"You're welcome, I'm sure. If you'll excuse me, I have to see to dinner." The woman bustled off down the hall, muttering to herself.

Liz entered a room of beautiful proportions with lemon-yellow taffeta at the high windows, soft green and multicolored chintz on the upholstered pieces, white rattan and polished wood tones. She looked around, expecting to see her hostess. There was no one there.

Grateful for a chance to compose herself, Liz put her case on the floor. She began a sigh of relief; it turned into a gasp. Entering the room through the French doors was one of the most extraordinary women Liz had ever seen. She was six feet tall if she was an inch, and her raven-black hair was piled atop her head and pierced with intricately carved chopsticks, making her look even taller. Her island dress, in flamboyant hues of apricot, fuchsia and tangerine, was made of drifty and flowing fabric, and around her neck was a chunky, barbaric collar of gold.

And her bones... good grief, what bones. Liz's fingers itched for her camera. She could only stare as the creature came toward her, hands outstretched, with a warm, welcoming smile in her hazel eyes.

"Elizabeth, my dear, I'm Sondra Hogan. We're so glad you're here." She took in Liz's appearance. "But what on earth has happened to you?"

As Mrs. Hogan came closer, Liz noted that there were a few streaks of silver in her hair and faint lines around her eyes. But even those gentle signs of age didn't explain the discrepancy. Fran Mason of the Hawaii Visitors' Bureau, the friend of her parents who had contracted with Liz for this job, had also made the arrangements for her to stay with Mrs. Hogan and her son. Mrs. Mason had said that she and Sondra Hogan were in school together.

Fran Mason had tightly curled gray hair and wore sensible shoes.

This woman had a shape like a goddess and moved like a girl. Liz imagined that she would deep-six any pair of sensible shoes that dared show up in her closet. "You are Mrs. Hogan?" she asked blankly, forgetting to answer the question directed at her.

Sondra Hogan laughed, the sound exuberant and rich. "Yes, but please call me Sondra."

"Forgive me for staring." Liz stammered her apology. "You're so young." Finally she remembered her manners. "And thank you for having me."

"Don't apologize, my dear. I'm flattered beyond words. Come and sit down," said Sondra, leading the way to a lovely sofa. "Are you really all right? We expected you earlier."

Liz sank wearily into the sofa and looked at her ruined suit. "I would have been here earlier, but I got lost and backed my rental car into a ditch," she said with a wry smile. "I walked the rest of the way."

Sondra looked at her, horrified. "Walked? From where?"

"From the road that leads to the south pasture," said a deep voice from the French doors behind them.

Liz turned to see another extraordinary person. Evidently there was no room for commonplace human beings on the island of Hawaii. She had an impression of masculinity carved from unyielding marble and whipcord strength, of brooding, hooded eyes.

Again she felt the craving for her camera. Squinting through a lens was her choice method for observing, and he would make a great study.

This must be the son. He was taller than Sondra but as perfectly shaped for a man as she was for a woman. He was broad-shouldered, lean-hipped and long-legged. His blue chambray shirt and jeans were covered with dust. He was in sharp contrast with this very elegant room. The upper part of his face was shadowed by a sweat-stained Stetson, but his jaw was square and strong.

Sondra's smile was immediate. "Justin, come here. You remember Elizabeth Ennis, the photographer friend of Fran Mason's who's going to be staying with us for a while."

It was an odd introduction. The man looked at Liz for a long, silent minute, seeming to wait for a reaction. Liz was at a loss. There was something familiar about him. But, no, she told herself. If she'd met this man before she would remember. "How do you do, Mr. Hogan?"

Sondra looked at her in surprise, and a muscle in Justin Hogan's jaw jumped. Then he exchanged a glance with his mother and shrugged. "How do you do, Miss Ennis?" he answered. His voice was dark and husky.

It was not a friendly greeting, and Liz wondered why. Maybe he didn't like visitors. She tried to make sense, too, of the exchange between mother and son. She chose to ignore his cool tone, at least until she discovered the reason for it.

"Did you find Elizabeth's car?" Sondra asked.

"Yes, we found it," said Justin. He didn't add that, though the car wasn't damaged, his heart had lodged in his throat until he'd walked in here and seen that Liz Ennis was safe. He planted his feet and slid his hands in the pockets of his jeans.

So, she didn't remember him. He shouldn't be surprised; she'd made it clear their meeting was less than momentous. When he'd met her a year ago, he'd rated her quickly as a shallow, haughty woman. The curious thing about her was, however, that her personality was so at odds with her talent.

He'd first seen her photographs in *Geography Today* two years ago. He'd been a fan of hers since then.

Her pictures were emotionally provoking and often severely sensitive. The images didn't balance.

"Justin, take off that hat. Why did you come in this way without cleaning up first?" his mother chided, recalling him from his thoughts.

"I've been working, Mother," he said dryly.

Liz watched the hard mouth soften slightly into a patient expression that was not quite a smile. "I just stopped in to tell Miss Ennis that I've sent one of the men with the Jeep to pull her car out of the ditch." He turned toward Liz, the smile—if that's what it was—fading. "Someone will bring your luggage to the house in ten minutes or so."

"Thank you, Mr. Hogan."

"And dinner will be in an hour," his mother reminded him. "Go clean up and take off that hat in the house."

"I'm on my way."

Liz watched him go, amused by the exchange but puzzled by his coolness toward her. She wondered if he was like this to all his mother's guests or if he just didn't like her in particular. Maybe she had come at a busy time; maybe he was tired. She also noticed that the hat remained on his head. His mother's admonitions had about as much effect as a gnat on an elephant's hide. She might be the woman of the house, but this was one man who did exactly as he pleased. When he left, some of the vitality seemed to drain out of the room.

Sondra rose with a sigh of exasperation. "That boy! You'd think he'd never been taught good manners."

Liz stood, too, and bit her lower lip to conceal her grin. The idea of the six-foot-plus and past-thirty man being called a boy was comical, and Liz doubted seriously that Justin Hogan ever let a lack of manners worry him.

"I'm sure, after your mishap, you would appreciate a hot bath as well, Elizabeth. Come with me and I'll show you to your room."

Liz picked up her camera case and followed Sondra up a graceful curving staircase. "Thank you. I would like a bath."

"I've really looked forward to having you here, Elizabeth. I miss female companionship since my daughter married and moved to the mainland. When Justin marries or my daughter decides to give me a grandchild, I shall probably move there, too, but I stay for now to keep him from becoming a complete barbarian and recluse."

"He doesn't seem the reclusive type," offered Liz tentatively into the expectant silence. She wouldn't have touched the other with a ten-foot pole.

"No, he doesn't give that impression, does he? But it's true. I was hoping—"

Sondra closed her mouth deliberately, cutting off her statement as they reached the top of the stairs. This hall, a counterpart to the one below, had gleaming hardwood floors protected at random by jewel-toned Oriental runners. Sondra turned right and led the way past three doors. At the fourth, she paused to let Liz precede her.

The bedroom was decorated in creamy white with accents of pink and rose. The beautiful tester bed was draped in a woven gossamer fabric and heaped with a profusion of pillows from the lightest to the darkest shades of the accent colors. The carpet was a dusty rose, as was an inviting chaise longue covered in crisp moire. White plantation shutters were pushed away from open doors, letting in the fragrant air and a spectacular view of the gardens below. In the distance the Pacific Ocean was losing its color to twilight.

Sondra looked around as though to assure herself that everything was in place. "I'll leave you to rest for a while before dinner. Your luggage will be up soon but there's a robe in the bath if you want a shower before it arrives. If you need anything else, just ring this bell and Annie will take care of you. I hope you'll be comfortable here."

"I'm sure I'll be very comfortable," she said, masking her amusement. If Sondra Hogan had seen where she'd been sleeping until a week ago, she would have been shocked. The barren deserts of Northern Africa didn't provide luxury like this.

When Sondra had gone Liz dropped the heavy camera case on the bed, kicked off her ruined shoes and wandered out onto the balcony. She spread her arms, rested her hands on the cool wrought iron and released a long, relieved sigh. The balcony looked out over a lush garden. A huge banyan tree stood guard nearby. It must have been standing there for hundreds of years. She put her head back and inhaled deeply. The sun had set, and the scene before her was diminished by the twilight, but the air-borne scents were wonderful. Another vivid contrast from her last assignment.

She seldom took commissions like this one, but she had met Fran Mason several times during her visits to the islands and liked her very much. When the Visitors' Bureau needed new photos of the Big Island, where the Hawaiian people had first settled, they'd wanted a different slant. Fran had explained that they were anxious to emphasize the character and historical culture of the island as well as the beauty. She had offered Liz the job, making the offer a challenge.

As the twilight deepened to darkness, a chain of lights in the distance identified the coastal highway. Liz felt her weariness drain away. She decided she'd done the right thing by coming here.

Liz had been hesitant about accepting—the job wasn't her usual style—but then in a telephone conversation with her parents, her mother had mentioned that Liz's ex-fiancé had been transferred to Japan.

Still, she wasn't quite sure why she *had* decided to return to the islands, except that she hadn't seen her folks in a year. And she recognized the need for some beauty in her life. Her cameras had been focused for so long on the gritty and the sullen that perhaps a temporary change would give her work fresh dimension.

Earlier, before she'd entered the house, she'd experienced an uncanny sensation. It wasn't just the obvious luxury of Fairwinds; the place had a presence, a confidence of its own, that caught her attention and appealed to her imagination. Her first glimpse had been of a building bathed in lovely golden light. Its wings, like extended arms, were open and welcoming. Her steps had quickened involuntarily as she drew near. She was eager to study the property at other times of day, to see if she could catch its surprising ambience on film.

The only thing that hadn't suffered from her fiancé's deceit was her work. Not many things had been able to stir her in the year since her broken engagement. But this house did.

She'd been standing on the balcony for about fifteen minutes when a knock on the door of the bedroom brought her out of her reverie. "Come in." She spoke over her shoulder. "Just put them anywhere, please. I'll unpack later."

Silence greeted her words. After a minute, when a peculiar instinct warned her that she was being watched, she jerked her head around. Justin Hogan stood a few feet away, hands in his pockets, one shoulder propped against the door jamb. The carpet must have muffled his footsteps.

He had showered and changed very quickly. Now he was dressed in a white-on-white island shirt and black trousers. His dark hair was still wet. His face was in shadow but she felt his compelling gaze like a caress on her body. His examination was thorough and—she decided—rather obvious, as his eyes roamed over her, taking in every aspect from her untidy hair to her bare feet, lingering longest on her legs.

Annoyed, Liz turned to lean against the balcony rail. So he wanted to play sensual games, did he? Well, she'd learned long ago how to handle men like him.

She crossed her arms and subjected him to a study of her own. Broad shoulders, lean hips—her earlier impression of undiluted masculinity was only reinforced.

Surprisingly, something deep and feminine within her responded. The visual exchange set off a warning bell in her brain: if this were allowed to develop into a contest, she was very much afraid she was looking at the winner.

It was he who broke the silence. "I brought your luggage," he informed her, a trace of amusement in his voice.

"Thank you," she responded calmly, though her heartbeat had accelerated. She could see tiny droplets of water reflecting in his hair like a halo through the light behind him. A halo? She almost laughed aloud. She couldn't conceive a less likely candidate for a halo.

Still he didn't move. "How did you happen to be on that road?" he asked.

"It wasn't by choice, I assure you. I was looking for your plantation or ranch—what do you call it?"

There was a hint of activity at a corner of his mouth. She waited expectantly, but the smile never fully materialized. "We call it a ranch."

"Well." She shrugged, wondering if he *ever* smiled. "Whatever. The road isn't very well marked and I got stuck on that dead end."

"The road isn't marked at all. We discourage casual visitors to the house. Didn't Fran Mason give you directions?"

Liz didn't want to admit that she'd barely listened to them. That was her first day in Hawaii in the twelve months since her broken engagement, and her emotions had been in a turmoil. There were too many memories to conquer for her to concentrate fully, but she thought she'd gotten the gist. "I misunderstood her."

"Your car is okay except for a mud bath. You didn't even dent a fender. It will be cleaned and ready for you in the morning."

"Thank you," she said again with difficulty. She didn't know why she found it so hard to express her gratitude to this man. He had been accommodating, bringing her bags, arranging for her car to be towed out of the ditch. And yet she doubted that kindness had any part in his motivation. His attitude downstairs certainly hadn't been kind. She wished he would leave.

"You don't remember our having met before?"

That *was* a surprise. "We've met?" Her brows knit in a frown. "No, I don't think so."

"Why?"

"Because—" She hesitated. *Because you're not the kind of man a woman would forget.* Something told her she shouldn't admit that. "I'm usually good at remembering people."

His short laugh was more like a bark. "I'm crushed," he said sarcastically. "And you almost fainted in my arms, too."

Her back straightened. "I've never fainted in my life," she answered tightly, frowning at the shadowed planes of his face.

But suddenly her frown deepened. A man...his eyes fixed on her, a sarcastic tone of voice.... On impulse she rose and brushed past him into the bedroom, forcing him to turn, to face the light. As soon as she saw the emerald-green gaze, her own eyes closed for a minute as it all came back to her. That night, the climax of that horrible day, he'd been at the party at her parents' quarters...

She had been right. Except under any but the most overwhelming circumstances she would never have forgotten this man. But now recollection of their meeting a year ago came rushing back. She had been devastated, had wanted nothing more than to crawl into some dark place to hide like a wounded animal. Instead, she had arrived at the admiral's house to find a sizable cocktail party in progress. To add to her agony, Justin Hogan had been unforgivably cavalier.

But then, so had she.

She opened her eyes reluctantly. "I remember now," she admitted. "I'm surprised I didn't recognize you immediately." Since her return to Hawaii, the whole sordid mess with Taylor—having to call off the wedding, return the gifts, make vague explanations—had been on her mind. And this man was very much a part of that day.

He gave her a moment then spoke again. "You didn't get married after all."

"Obviously not."

He turned his back to the door jamb and crossed his arms over his chest. He looked very big, very forbidding. His magnetism reached out like the tentacles of an octopus, she decided, pleased at the fitting simile.

"I wonder why," he said in a conversational tone. "Your parents were discussing the wedding before you arrived that evening. They seemed pleased that you had chosen a man they'd known for a long time, and a naval officer as well. From what your father said, I gathered it was the perfect match."

"It didn't turn out that way."

"I knew something was wrong with you when we were introduced. You turned as white as a sheet. At first I thought you might be—"

"Pregnant?" she interrupted. "Yes, you mentioned that. I'd really prefer not to discuss it."

He was silent, as though trying to decide whether to persist. She prayed silently that he wouldn't.

Just then Annie walked by the open door to the hall. "Justin, there you are. There's a phone call for you from that breeder in Texas."

"Thanks, Annie. I'll be right there." He levered his long body away from the door. "I'm still very curious, you know," he said. "Maybe you're not the little snob you appeared to be that night." He stopped when he was even with her and looked into her eyes, his own dark with a mysterious energy. "You told me very flatly that you were bored with my company."

The charge of boredom rankled, Liz realized. "I'm sorry." She almost smiled. Justin Hogan would arouse a lot of emotions, but boredom would certainly not be one of them. However, she wouldn't tell him that; he was too sure of himself. Let him wonder.

Suddenly he touched her cheek, lightly, briefly, with just the tips of his fingers. The effect was electrifying. All her satisfaction dissipated.

"Maybe I can change your mind," he said in a low, sexy voice that sent chills over her scalp. "See you at dinner." He turned his back on her.

Change her mind? Liz went to the bed and sat carefully on its edge. Round one had not gone well. She'd entered the fray without thinking things through. Therefore, she had become a challenge to him. As the object of his determination, she was not in an enviable position. She sighed heavily and flopped back on the mattress.

To be fair, she supposed she owed him a partial explanation of that night a year ago, if only to soothe his ego. Perhaps then he would back off.

Chapter Two

Steam rose from the large tub as Liz helped herself to bath salts. The smell of jasmine mingled pleasantly with the steam. She undressed and slid into the hot water, releasing a sigh of pleasure as she felt the tension aroused by Justin Hogan begin to ease.

Ten minutes. That's all it would take. Ten minutes to relax and get her thoughts in order. Then she could face him with aplomb. She would explain about that night a year ago. She couldn't be comfortable staying in his home otherwise.

Liz had made a promise to herself after the breakup of her engagement. She'd made several—a lot of them in bitterness; those, she had long since forsworn. But the most important was, instead of being a problem solver, she was going to learn to be the kind of person who avoided problems by not letting them develop in the first place. She had become a master at side-stepping trouble.

Justin Hogan could be trouble. He was all male and aware of it. She'd met his type before, she reminded herself, remembering his visual inventory very clearly indeed. The sort of man who couldn't look at a woman without a sensual evaluation, he had confidence that his interest would be returned. If he wanted it to be.

Well, she wasn't susceptible to that kind of man; she never had been. But she readily recognized the danger in him, and surely recognition was the most important step to self-protection.

A short time later, Liz, much refreshed, paused over her wardrobe. She always traveled light. When she was working, her needs were slight—jeans, khakis, shorts and comfortable tops. If a situation arose where she needed appropriate dress, she could always go out and buy something. This time, on a stopover to see her parents, her mother had suggested she include a few of the intended honeymoon outfits that had lain fallow in a storage closet for a year.

At first Liz had protested, not even wanting to *see* the clothes that had been selected with the happy idea of pleasing her ex-fiancé. Her mother, however, in the quiet, persistent way that was so characteristic of her, had convinced Liz of the practicality of wearing the clothes.

Liz shook her head at the memory. If her father was right, she had inherited her mother's talent. He had always said she could talk anyone into anything. She wasn't sure about the absolutes, but more than once, she had been able to talk her way into areas other photographers couldn't get near.

As she dressed in a pretty sundress, she thought she noticed a bit of expectation in her eyes that hadn't been there this morning. She leaned forward to check more closely in the mirror. Her skin glowed, but the color was simply a reflection of the peach silk. A shiver ran across her bare shoulders. Dismissing the changes in herself, she made her way downstairs.

Her step did not falter when she saw that Justin was alone in the drawing room. She resolved to be friendly. Period. She wouldn't see him that much after she got herself organized. She could arrange her schedule to make sure of that.

"May I fix you something?" he asked. His tone was pleasant but his eyes swept over her in a way that she was beginning to recognize as routine.

Her reaction to it was becoming predictable, as well, she thought wryly. She tingled. "Sherry, please."

He indicated several bottles. "Dry? Sweet?"

She lifted her shoulders and sat in a pretty wing chair. "It doesn't matter."

"I'm surprised. I would have thought you were a woman who had definite ideas about what she wanted."

"I've learned not to coddle my tastes. In some of the places I've worked, it pays to be flexible."

"Yes, I've seen your work. You're good."

Liz was accustomed to more effusive compliments on her work, but his simple words warmed her because she had an idea that he didn't hand out compliments indiscriminately. "Thank you."

He went on, "The photo essay in India that you did for *Geography Today* two years ago was excellent work. I still have my copy."

She smiled. "I'm going back for a follow-up assignment soon, probably when I finish here. I'm waiting to hear from the editor."

Without comment he poured her sherry and brought it to her. She took the delicate stemmed glass and the linen napkin he offered. He took a chair at right angles to hers. They were quiet for a minute.

This room was more formal than the morning room, a shade more masculine, but equally comfortable. The colors were warm saffron and burgundy; the fabrics, soft, supple damasks with muted patterns and silky satin stripes. Liz looked around as she searched her mind for a way to introduce the subject of their meeting last year. She cleared her throat.

"Justin."

Justin met her eyes, elevated a dark brow and waited.

Liz shifted slightly and sipped from her glass. "Justin," she repeated.

He chuckled. "Are you nervous, Liz?" he asked smoothly.

Her glance was keen but she could read no sign of sarcasm in his expression. "Maybe I am," she admitted. "I was thinking earlier—my dad used to say I could talk to anyone about anything, but this is very difficult." She set down her glass and linked her fingers together in her lap.

"I would like to explain about my behavior at the party last year." She shook her head and gave a deprecating laugh. "I can't believe I actually told you that I was bored. I apologize. But, you see . . ." She took a deep breath. She had fully recovered from her broken engagement. If she'd doubted before, this trip proved that to her. But still she didn't like to talk about an event that had been humiliating as well as heartbreaking.

Intrigued, Justin leaned forward in his chair, propping his elbows on his knees and turning his glass between his palms. She had his full attention.

"My fiancé—" Liz broke off, her eyes going to a spot on the wall above his head. How should she put this in order to delete the humiliating parts? "My engagement ended that day, that afternoon. I was distressed . . . to put it mildly," she said with a wry smile as she met his gaze.

It was easier to continue after that. "I barely remember driving from Honolulu to Barber's Point. I'm not even sure how I got there. All I could think of was reaching my parents. And when I arrived I stepped into the middle of a party. I tried to behave naturally; I couldn't deal with the questions an announcement would have provoked. Not right then. It was—'' she searched for a word "—hard.''

There was no mistaking the sincerity and self-disgust when he said, "And then I came on like a— God, I'm sorry." His voice sounded hollow.

She had begun to unwind, relieved that her explanation and apology were over; but, at his words, her backbone straightened, her chin rose. "I wasn't asking for pity," she interrupted, her voice sharp.

Justin held up a hand. "I didn't mean I was sorry for you. I meant I'm sorry I acted like such an ass."

She relented. "You couldn't have known. Anyway, again, I'm sorry I was so rude to you."

Justin set his glass on the table between them and adjusted his chair to a better angle. His green eyes fixed on her, then looked away. He wasn't sure how to put this. She was right about one thing—no one would have known from her bearing that she was upset that day.

For several years, Justin had supplied prime beef to the military clubs throughout the islands. A year ago, when he had been on Oahu on business, he'd met the admiral and been invited to the party. It had been just another commercial trip mellowed by a pleasant social occasion.

Until she walked into the room. Tall and beautiful, she had moved with a queenly grace absent in many women. Her hair was the flame of Pele, the volcano goddess. Her eyes—when they met his—were the aquamarine color of the seas around the islands, exotically shaped and hypnotizing. Desire had never hit him so suddenly. He felt as though the floor had dropped from under his feet.

Now he met her clear aquamarine eyes. "Let me tell you something about that day, Liz. I'm not wild about parties. My mother is the social one in the family. But that one was business mixed with pleasure.

"I was talking to your father when I looked up to see this gorgeous redhead walk in. I was immediately—interested." He cringed inwardly at the understatement. "I opened my mouth to ask him to introduce me, but before I could get the words out, I discovered you were the daughter with the wedding plans. It made me mad as hell, and I overreacted."

Liz listened to him with growing astonishment. Her looks were not something she took seriously. When she checked her appearance in a mirror, what she saw was a tall, clumsy teenager, wearing horrible thick horn-rimmed glasses and braces on her teeth, and towering over her classmates. She couldn't help it; she laughed.

A forbidding scowl descended on his brow. "Do you think it's funny that I found you attractive?"

She shook her head and fought to regain her composure. "No, I'm not laughing at you. Not at all. I think it's wonderful and very flattering. No, I only wish I'd known your reaction that night. I would have felt a whole lot better." Her smile was warm, inviting him to share her amusement.

Justin felt his smile expand in response. This luscious, long-legged goddess was irresistible. From the first minute he'd laid eyes on her, though he'd thought her a well-bred snob, he'd nonetheless been fascinated. And that night, when he realized that she belonged to someone else, he wanted to put a fist through the wall. It was only later that he discovered who she was professionally and wondered at the discrepancy between her pictures and her personality.

But now she was free. Or he assumed she was. "Are you involved with anyone else?" he asked.

She laughed again. "Not a chance. I've learned my lesson."

Justin picked up his glass, hooked an arm over the back of his chair and took a swallow of his Scotch, feeling very satisfied. Have you? he thought. "Really?" He could change her mind.

The word was thrown out so casually, so mildly, that Liz almost missed the renewed challenge there. She opened her mouth to set him straight, but just then Sondra came into the room, and she had to be content with a glare that clearly denied him the assumption. A few moments later Annie announced dinner.

Shining mahogany reflected the luminescence of a dozen candles set into ornate silver. At one end of the table, three places were set with cutwork mats and napkins. Centered on plates were individual crystal compotes of colorful fruit.

Justin seated his mother on his right and Liz on his left. She looked up to find herself staring into Justin's vivid green eyes in a portrait above the sideboard. "Good heavens!" she said without thinking.

Sondra followed her gaze. "Justin is very like his father, isn't he?" She smiled and picked up her spoon.

The resemblance was startling. The strong, determined jaw, the dark curly hair, and of course the eyes were identical. The only differences as far as she could see were in age and in the mouth. Justin's father's lips were thinner, not as sensual.

When she looked from the portrait to his mouth, Justin caught her making the comparison and smiled. His expression was a great deal too astute, reminding her of the exchange Sondra's arrival had interrupted. He was an appealing man, very sexy. If she were open to an intimate affair, she would be flattered by his interest; but she wasn't. She would have to convince him of that.

Between the penetrating eyes of the portrait and the real ones to her right, Liz was on edge for the rest of the meal.

Sondra kept up a conversation, thank goodness, and Liz found that they had traveled to many of the same places. At times during the small talk, she could almost forget the green gaze that often wandered to her face. Later, over coffee served at the table, Justin happened to mention Liz's father.

Sondra looked at her son then at Liz. "Then you did remember meeting before?" she asked.

Liz held her breath, but Justin handled the explanation very smoothly.

"I wondered about that," said Sondra. "When Justin suggested that we invite you to stay here, I had the impression that you'd known each other fairly well."

Justin suggested? Liz's gaze shot to him. So, he was the one who had decided that she should stay here, not Fran Mason. She wondered why. She'd been rude, told him he was a bore—why in the world would he want her in his home? She didn't like the sudden feeling that she was being manipulated.

But Sondra had moved on to the subject of places on the island that Liz should see. "Justin has a large, detailed map on the wall of his study," she was saying. "After dinner he can point out some of his favorite haunts. One of the sights you must see is Akaka Falls by moonlight."

Liz fumbled through the warning bells that were still going off in her brain to find a lucid answer for Sondra. She was familiar with photographs of the waterfall, which dropped off a cliff into a gorge over four-hundred feet below.

The one thing that had kept her going over the past year was her love of her job, and this was an exciting prospect. She turned her full attention to the older woman. Her enthusiasm was reflected in her smile. "I've seen pictures of the falls, of course, but I don't think I've seen any by moonlight. The island has been photographed so often and so well that it won't be easy to find a different perspective, but that's the kind of thing I'll be searching for.''

She didn't notice that both Sondra and Justin were looking at her as though they'd never seen her before. ''The falls is near here, isn't it?''

Sondra cleared her throat. ''Yes,'' she said, her voice sounding slightly choked. ''It's not far away, only about a half-hour by Jeep.''

Justin had caught his breath, bobbled his cup and almost splashed hot coffee into his lap at Liz's sudden metamorphosis. In her excitement and animation, she had turned from a self-possessed beauty to a vibrant one. Good Lord! She was more than beautiful, she was breathtaking, magnificent. Silently, but vehemently, he cursed the man who had robbed her of this vitality, this animation, however temporary.

He frowned. This unforeseen aspect of Liz Ennis put a whole new light on his intentions. She looked younger, more vulnerable. This Liz wasn't a woman with whom you had a brief, fleeting affair. This was the kind of woman you made commitments to. He was attracted to her, he told himself, but not to that extent. He'd have to rethink this situation.

Liz was asking his mother a question. ''Akaka Falls is a state park, isn't it? Could I get permission to shoot at night?''

''I'll make the arrangements and take you there myself,'' he said brusquely.

Her excitement faded at the unexpected hostility in his voice, and she introduced a corresponding chill in her answer. "Thanks anyway. I can probably get the permission myself." Or Fran Mason can, she added silently.

"I said I'd take you," he said sharply.

Liz felt her irritation grow. She had no idea what had happened between one minute and the next to cause his mood swing, but she hadn't forgotten his mother's remark.

Quickly, to change the subject, Sondra said, "By the way, Justin, I'm arranging a dinner party for next Saturday night. Black tie. So please don't make any other plans."

Justin made an impatient sound. "Damn it, Mother, I have to leave for Texas the following Monday. Do you realize how busy I'll be that weekend?"

"Don't curse, Justin," Sondra said, in what Liz realized was an automatic admonishment, one that didn't require a response. "Please," she added plaintively. "It won't be a big party."

He rose. "All right, Mother," he said wearily, his brows marred by a frown. "If you'll both excuse me, I have some work to do."

Liz read his reluctance as though she were thumbing through a familiar novel. Socializing often got in the way of family matters, as she well knew.

If she hadn't been so annoyed with him she could have sympathized, remembering the times she had come home seeking comfort and, instead, was faced with a party. She had the impression that Justin tolerated such affairs, just as she had always done, but didn't really enjoy them. At this moment, however, she could only feel grateful that she was about to be relieved of his presence.

"Of course you may be excused, dear," said Sondra. "Take Elizabeth along with you and show her the map. She can decide where she wants to go tomorrow."

"If Justin has work to do I can see it later." Liz definitely didn't want to be alone with him again.

"Nonsense. It will only take a minute. Go on," Sondra persisted.

Silently, they left the dining room. They walked side by side down the broad hallway until they reached the staircase. At that point Liz turned. She had a foot on the first step when he took her arm and pulled her back.

"My mother wants you to see the map," he said through clenched teeth.

"I'll see it later."

"I may be busy later. You'll see it now."

Liz deliberately raised a brow. "Why did you invite me to stay here?"

Instead of answering, his grip tightened and he propelled her down the hall and into a room opposite the morning room. He closed the door behind them.

His maneuver had been very quick and he was very strong. Other than screaming out her protest, she hadn't much choice but to go along. But once they were alone in the room and he had released her, she whirled to confront him. "I do not like to be man-handled, Hogan," she informed him in a low, dangerous tone. "And I can make my own plans without your map."

"Of course, you can. But we need to talk."

"I can't think of anything else we have to say. You're obviously a very busy man. Let's drop it, shall we?" She turned to go. As she reached for the door-knob he was there, his hands against the walnut panels on each side of her head. He didn't touch her but she was effectively hemmed in.

"Liz, I told you of my reaction the night we first met," he began.

She refused to turn. "I'm not interested," she said to the walnut panels.

"Not interested in what?" he asked smoothly.

"I'm not blind, Justin. In an affair, a romance, whatever it is you have on your mind."

For a moment, Justin was taken aback by her blunt honesty, but he quickly recovered. One side of his mouth lifted. He would have to be more careful. This was no air-headed beauty. "Liz, my mother is an active volunteer for the Visitors' Bureau as well as being a friend of Fran's. She—we often entertain visitors. When Fran called to say you would be doing the photography for their book, we agreed that you would benefit by staying with someone who knows the island well." He didn't add that he'd been the one to answer the phone, that the invitation had been a spur-of-the-moment thing, issued the minute he'd learned she hadn't married.

"And you had no intention of initiating anything more personal?"

Her perfume was as sophisticated and enticing as she was. Her bare shoulders were only inches from his lips. Justin let his head drop back and stared at the ceiling for a minute. Then he looked at the back of her head and sighed. "I won't lie to you."

"That's a comfort," she said shortly.

"Unfortunately, I can't seem to ignore you." He dipped his head to put his lips at the side of her neck. The kiss was very quick, fleeting.

His lips were warm. Liz hunched up her shoulder against their effect. "Stop that," she ordered, but her tone didn't hold the right degree of indifference. Her voice sounded tremulous even to her own ears.

"Why won't you look at me?" he asked. "I don't scare you, do I?"

Her shoulder relaxed. "A bit," she admitted. "I'm not good at games, Justin."

He dropped his head again. "Who said we were playing games?" he murmured against her bare shoulder.

"Then I'd better add that I haven't had a lot of ex-perience." She held her breath.

Justin was still for a minute. He was suddenly hit with an awful premonition. "Liz, are you a virgin?" he asked as he bent forward to watch her profile. She didn't have to answer. The rush of color that rose in her face did it for her.

He muttered something obscene and dropped his arms immediately. He strode to his desk, plunged his hands into his pockets and stood with his back to her, staring down. "I don't know anything about this fiancé of yours, but I can't understand why he didn't have you in his bed a year ago." His voice was harsh.

Liz turned and leaned against the door, watching him. His words had pricked at her heart. Her throat burned; she fought off the tears that threatened. "He didn't try. He found his diversion in other beds," she said woodenly.

Justin looked over his shoulder. He saw the one tear that had escaped despite her intentions. He returned to her side, moving more slowly now. One finger caught the moisture at the corner of her eye. He looked at it for a minute, his expression unreadable, then he rubbed his fingers together. The moisture evaporated instantly. "See? The tear is gone. Let that be the last one you shed for him, because the man is a damned fool," he said gruffly.

His offhand remark had an unexpected effect on her. A warmth that had nothing to do with his nearness stole into her very soul, melting the ice there, repairing her bruised pride without a scar. She realized all at once that her ego had taken far more of a beating than her heart.

A stray, irrelevant thought flickered through her mind then was lost, but not before she'd had a quick glimpse of it. The thought was—if only her pride was broken and not her heart, why had she gotten engaged in the first place? Mentally, she shook herself. "Thank you, Justin," she said in a quiet tone.

"For what?" he asked guardedly.

Her lips curved into a poignant smile. "I'm not quite sure. Maybe for making me feel like a woman again." Just in case he misunderstood her words, she rushed to add, "That doesn't mean I don't think we would be smart to keep things casual between us."

He continued to study her features for a moment. Then he sighed deeply and put a brotherly arm across her shoulders as he led her to a leather sofa. "Okay. Sit there," he said. "I'm going to help you plan your itinerary."

When Sondra came in a half-hour later, she found them poring over some old maps. Justin was saying, "Some of these places are accessible only on horseback. One place in particular is a favorite of mine, but it isn't easy to get to. You don't ride, do you, Liz?"

"I love to ride," she answered with a smile, noting his surprise. "Why did you assume I didn't?"

Justin tried to remember. Last night—what had she said? Something that gave him the impression she was unfamiliar with the ranch life-style. "I warn you. It won't be cantering over smooth pastures. It will be packhorses on mountain trails. Let's see—this week is pretty full for me. What about next weekend?"

"Don't forget my dinner party on Saturday night," said Sondra.

Justin nodded. "We'll go on Sunday."

"And I'll use the car this weekend to shoot some of the more obvious spots." Liz waved a list she had made while they talked.

"Well, I'm glad you got that settled. I'm going up to bed," Sondra told them.

Liz rose and stretched. "I'll go up with you, Sondra. Good night, Justin, and thanks again." Liz and Sondra left the room together.

"Justin calls you Liz," said Sondra as they started up the broad staircase.

"Yes, most people do."

"Then I shall, too." Sondra gave her a sideways look. "It fits you."

As their voices faded away, Justin sighed deeply. He crossed to a cabinet that held a small bar, poured himself a straight whiskey and downed it in one swallow. Then he sighed again.

For the next few days, the casual but friendly relationship between Justin and Liz held. Each night after dinner he took her into his study and they pored over the maps. He lent her books of Hawaiian history from his extensive collection and helped her plan her itinerary for the next day.

He casually but firmly avoided personal subjects and was careful not to touch her, taking a chair across the room if she settled into the leather cushions of the sofa and retreating behind his desk if she took the chair.

Liz was still very much aware of his masculine potency. Occasionally, as they talked, she would glance up to find his eyes fixed on her lips. Those moments visibly unnerved her, and he always deflected his gaze immediately. Though he must have noticed her reaction, he didn't take advantage. He continued to treat her like a younger sister.

Liz had arrived at Fairwinds on Friday night. Tuesday morning, she was downstairs early, dressed in white jeans and a sleeveless, V-necked top of Kelly green. In addition to her camera case, she was carrying a tote bag containing her bathing suit and a towel. She entered the kitchen swinging the bag as Justin was leaving by the back door.

He stopped to grin at her obvious good mood. "You're in luck. There's a full moon and I've made arrangements for us to go to the falls tonight," he said.

"Tonight?" She didn't know why she felt uneasy at the prospect.

"You may not have another night as perfect as this. What have you got in there?" he asked, pointing to the bag.

"My bathing suit. I might decide to play hooky today."

A frown appeared on his brow. "Don't swim alone, Liz. There's a lot of coral in the ocean around here. If you want to swim, why don't you use the pool?"

"I haven't seen a pool. Honestly, Justin, you sound just like James."

"Who the hell is James?" he growled.

"My brother." She poured herself a cup of coffee and turned to look at him from under long lashes.

The look he shot her was dangerous. "I remind you of your *brother?*" he asked, his voice low and challenging.

Liz was saved from having to answer by Annie. "Miss Ennis, I didn't know you were downstairs. What would you like for breakfast?"

Justin went out, muttering to himself. So she thought of him as a brother, huh? Maybe he should change that. Despite his efforts to keep things casual between them, he sure as hell didn't feel that way about her. Although he had to admit, things would be a damned sight easier if he did.

Liz bit back a smile as she watched him go. He didn't like being cast in the role of brother, that much was clear. But he had played it out with good grace. She was very grateful to him for that.

"Coffee is fine," she said in answer to Annie's question. "I want to get an early start. Will you please tell Mrs. Hogan that I won't be here for lunch, but I'll be back in plenty of time for dinner? See you later, Annie."

Justin's response had pleased her, and she left the house in a good mood. The past few days had been... interesting. Even though there had been few overt personal exchanges between them, there had been a lot of lively conversation and more than a few promising glances. He seemed to have shed some of his gritty reserve and had loosened up a bit.

She had even wondered—what would a small flirtation hurt? She'd be leaving before it had time to get complicated.

She was impressed by the depth of Justin's intelligence, and occasionally charmed by his sense of humor. Of course, as a gorgeous single man, he was twice as dangerous this way. Much, much too appealing, she reminded herself.

Chapter Three

At five o'clock that afternoon, Liz returned to find the house quiet. She took her equipment to her room, put on her bathing suit and went in search of a swimming pool.

She finally found it, some distance from the house and screened by a high hedge of hibiscus. From behind the dark green leaves that contrasted sharply with bright yellow blossoms, she heard the sound of splashing. She circled the hedge to find Sondra paddling happily in the shallow end. The pool was large and utilitarian, not at all what she would have expected in this home where every attention seemed to have been paid to beauty as well as comfort.

"Come join me," called the older woman.

Liz needed no urging; she dropped her cover-up and towel on a chair and dived in. She had tramped for miles, and the water felt cool and refreshing to her tired body. "This is heavenly," she said, turning onto her back and letting the water take her weight.

Sondra swam to the side of the pool and pulled herself out. "It is, isn't it? I don't swim as often as I used to but Justin uses it every day." She sat on the edge and leaned back, bracing herself on her hands and raising her face to the sun.

Liz was surprised. "Justin? When does he find the time?" It seemed to her that Justin worked from dawn to dark.

"He swims early in the morning. He and his father were always up to watch the sunrise." With a sweeping arm Sondra indicated the spectacular view to the east.

"It is a beautiful setting," said Liz. And it was. She wondered why there were no umbrellas, no tables and not much of an apron, just a pool and a couple of chairs. It didn't fit with the character of the rest of the house and grounds.

"Bill was an indulgent husband, with very few exceptions. But when we built this, I had envisioned a pretty pool set into the hillside near the lanai and decorated with lava rock and fountains. We could have had parties around it." She shook her head, sending droplets of water into the air.

"He thought that a pool should be large enough to swim laps without stubbing your toe. He constructed for exercise, not aesthetics." She wrinkled her nose. "I think the thing belongs in the YMCA, and I planted the hedge so I wouldn't have to look at it."

Liz laughed as she fanned her hands in the water to keep herself afloat. Sondra was delightful, a little spoiled but interesting.

Sondra stood and reached for a terry-cloth robe. She belted it around her slender waist and took a watch from the pocket. "Almost five-thirty. I suppose I'd better start dressing for dinner." Sondra made a face. "I don't know why we can't dine at a sophisticated hour, but Justin insists on eating early."

I can understand that, thought Liz, especially considering that he's up before dawn every morning. She was discovering that this ranch wasn't just a ranch in the clichéd sense of old Western movies. This was big business.

Liz swam toward the steps at the shallow end of the pool, intending to follow, but just then Justin came around the hedge dressed in swimming trunks.

He spoke to his mother and headed for the pool, snapping the towel from around his neck and dropping it on the grass. "Stay and swim with me," he urged with a smile. "I'll race you."

Standing in waist-deep water, Liz let her gaze travel the long height of him. His large body was even more impressive without clothes. She was rather surprisingly stirred by the sight of so much Justin. The muscles in his legs and arms were well defined and his shoulders looked even more broad. His chest was thick with dark curly hair that thinned to a silky arrow down his belly.

When her gaze reached the glittering green eyes, she realized that they were riveted on the thrust of her breasts. Though her suit was conservative, she suddenly felt naked. Her mouth was dry and her heartbeat accelerated alarmingly.

Justin seemed to recall himself. He sprinted toward the far end of the pool. "Ten laps, and I'll even give you a head start."

"I can't turn down such good odds." Relieved that the moment had passed, Liz pushed off from one end as he dived in from the other. She was a good swimmer, but his height and strength advantage made the winner a foregone conclusion. Still, she was pleased; it took him eight laps to catch her and when it was over he was breathing almost as hard as she was.

"Good race," he said. "Want to go again?"

Liz shook her head, treading water in front of him. "I know when I'm outclassed. I don't stand a chance against you."

Justin's smile faded as he looked at her. Her laughing eyes were slightly red from the chlorine. The water had darkened her auburn hair and slicked it away from her face. She had a faint sunburn across her nose and forehead. To him, she had never looked more beautiful.

She became aware of his intense scrutiny, and her lashes fell to half-cover her eyes. He was standing on the bottom, but she couldn't quite reach. She grabbed

for the edge of the pool but he intercepted her hand
and placed it on his shoulder.

"I'm beginning to think I don't stand a chance
against you, either," he said huskily.

She did not protest as he reached for her, his hand
at her waist drawing her forward until their legs
brushed under the water. The contact set off some
significant sensations within her body. "Justin, I don't
think—"

Her words were swallowed by his mouth. His arms
snaked around her, pulling her securely against his
wide chest. His kiss was hungry, demanding and unlike anything she'd experienced in her life. In response, her blood surged hot through her veins.

The water and Justin kept her upright. Even if she
could have touched bottom, she could not have stood
alone. She parted her lips and hugged his body, holding on as though he were the only stable thing in an
unstable world.

Slowly he loosened his arms, giving her time to ad-
just. But his eyes remained fixed on hers. "Shall we set
aside those sensible resolutions we made?" he asked.
There was a slight flush on his face and he sounded as
unsteady as she felt. One hand moved restlessly over
her back.

She fought the heated surge that had not ebbed
when the kiss ended and injected a light note into her
breathless question as she moved out of his arms.
"What are you talking about?" She grasped the con-
crete coping.

"Mine was, 'She's a very sexy woman but it wouldn't be smart to get involved.'" As though he couldn't bear not to touch her, he ran a finger down the side of her neck, idly, lazily.

Her eyes drifted shut; she couldn't fight her involuntary response.

"Don't tell me you didn't make one, too. What was it?" he added in a rough voice. His callused finger wandered lower to trace the top of her swimsuit, grazing the curves of her breasts. That snapped her eyes open.

She looked away. "Um. Something along the same lines," she admitted, moving hand over hand until she could stand. "They were probably good resolutions. I'm afraid I'm in over my head."

Justin planted his feet and watched as she edged away. Hell, she was as skittish as a newborn colt. What had he said? "How old are you, anyway?" he demanded.

"I'll be twenty-five next month."

He muttered a word that stopped her movement and widened her eyes. "That should be old enough."

"Enough for what?" she asked tightly.

"Enough to understand that I don't plan to take advantage of your innocence," he said, his tone heavy with irony. "You can relax." Before she could answer, he turned abruptly and hit the water. He swam toward the far end of the pool.

Lord, she'd made a fool of herself again. Moving as though submerged in a tub of molasses, Liz climbed out of the pool. She made her way to the chair where she'd left her cover-up and towel and dried herself as he swam several more laps. She tried not to stare at the powerful way his legs propelled him along and the strength of his arms as they bit into the water.

As she watched, she thought of that first night and Justin lounging against the door jamb of her balcony, casually inspecting her. Then later, in the study... her shoulder itched with the memory of his lips there, his warm breath. Odd that she'd been unaware of her neck and shoulders as erogenous places until she'd encountered Justin Hogan.

Well, she conceded, they were both unattached, young, healthy adults, weren't they? This morning, she'd dallied with the idea of flirtation, hadn't she? He was absolutely right; she was old enough.

But the kiss they'd just shared defied the definition of a mild anything and certainly moved them beyond the relaxed companionship they'd practiced since Friday night. She drew her gaze away. Flirtation aside, she much preferred the brotherly spirit, she decided.

Liz was lying on her towel, soaking up the last rays of the sun and letting her hair dry, when Justin climbed out of the pool. He grabbed for a towel, wiped his face and slung the towel around his neck. Then he stood over her, water dripping from the rest of him.

Sitting up abruptly, she squealed. "You're getting me wet again!" she accused, laughing.

The strenuous exercise hadn't relieved his physical ache. "You won't melt," he responded gruffly. *Not like others I've known,* he added to himself. This was a strong woman. He was annoyed with himself for baiting her, but it had been hard to keep his hands off her these past few days. Even now he couldn't seem to remove his gaze from the thrust of her breasts against her swimsuit.

And she caught him at it. She moved casually, reaching for her cover-up. "We'd better go in. I'll have to hurry to finish drying my hair and be dressed by dinnertime."

He let go of one end of the towel and reached down to help her to her feet. She came up very close to him. He held on to her fingers, looking down into her upturned face. Another deep shudder of desire went through his body and he set his back teeth together hard, fighting to control his need. Not much of his condition would be left to the imagination in this bathing suit. He pushed her away slightly and reached for the belt of her robe, fastening it with clumsy fingers.

Liz was tempted to touch him but didn't dare. She felt limp and stiff, warm and cold, all the way through, but her voice was soft. "Justin, I—"

Her soft tone jolted him. "Don't say anything," he barked.

She watched his face; a muscle jumped in his jaw. There was something very dangerous in the electricity between them.

Justin tightened the knot he'd made, then met her eyes, his own alight with anger, anger that was directed solely at himself. "Don't look at me like that."

Liz didn't know that, however. *"Okay,"* she replied promptly. She bent to scoop up her towel and headed for the house. He followed her around the hedge.

"Liz, I'm trying to go easy with you," he warned.

She whirled to face him, her own anger sharpening every line of her body. "Easy?" she said mildly. "Is that what you call it? Giving me orders like a drill sergeant? Don't do this, don't do that." She was trying very hard not to overreact, but her agitation demanded some kind of action, some physical release. She slapped the towel to his chest; his reaction was automatic—he grabbed it. She turned and marched toward the house, her temper, her emotions in a turmoil.

Justin caught up with her at the foot of the stairs. He touched her arm, stopping her headlong flight.

"Don't touch me," she cried, jerking her arm away.

He stopped. She stared in amazement at his rueful grin. Her anger faded away; hers was a lamentable excuse for a smile. "I'm doing it, too, aren't I? Sorry."

Justin was sorry, too. Clearly the feelings between the two of them were volatile, had been the whole time he'd been working so hard to control his. Every time he got close enough to smell her perfume he wanted to reach out and touch her. He was in a constant state of near-arousal, like a teenager whose hormones have just begun to function.

They started up the steps. "You're a very sexy woman," he said unwillingly.

Liz was stunned by his assessment. "*I* am?"

"After the kiss we just shared, you know damn well you are," he grated.

"Before that, though...well, you've been acting rather brotherly."

"Correction. *Trying* to act brotherly." He sighed. "If you weren't innocent the solution would be clear-cut."

"Here?"

He shot her a glance and laughed, but there was no humor in the sound. "There are ways. I have—" He had a beach cottage that he used when he wanted to get away, but he wasn't going to tell *her* that. "As it is...." He shrugged.

Liz refused to apologize for her lack of experience. She lifted her chin. "As it is, I could move to a hotel."

"No," he said immediately.

They had reached her door. She paused with her hand on the knob and raised her gaze to his. "Maybe it would be the best thing."

"No," he repeated. "I want you here." Then he shook his head, raked his fingers through his hair in a gesture of regret. "God, that sounds arrogant."

"Yes, it does," she agreed without rancor. She didn't take offense. Most of the successful men she'd known, her father included, had plenty of the self-confidence that occasionally deviated into arrogance. A man who could admit to such a characteristic usually controlled it readily. And the truth was she didn't want to leave.

"Anyway, don't ever confuse me with your brother again."

She caught her lower lip between her teeth to keep a laugh from escaping. "No, I won't," she assured him finally.

"Don't forget, we're going to the falls tonight," he said as she opened the door to her room.

She hesitated. After what had just happened between them, she knew it wouldn't be a good idea to be alone with him, especially in the moonlight....

Nonsense, she told herself. She was here to do a job. This was the best night to do it, and so she would. "Okay." Her answer sounded grudging.

"We'll leave after dinner." He looked at her hard but when she made no further protest, he strode off down the hall.

Liz watched his retreating back. Finally she roused herself and headed for the shower.

Justin glanced at his watch and said, "We'd better get going." He pushed back from the dinner table.

Liz touched her napkin to her mouth and stood. "I suppose I should change my clothes."

Justin's gaze roamed briefly over her bare shoulders. "Definitely," he agreed.

When he grinned at her Liz felt her heart pick up speed again. "Don't you want to go with us, Sondra?"

"Of course not. I don't hike," she said with a certain hauteur. Justin and Liz traded covert grins.

The drive passed quickly. Liz asked about the history of some of the places she'd seen and shot today. "Hawaii is a beautiful island—sometimes I feel like I'm going to O.D. on beauty. And sometimes I feel that I'm just not right for this job. Maybe I'm afraid what I'm doing is exploitation."

"Why did you take the job? It's not in your usual style, is it?"

Liz's brow furrowed in attempt to understand why she had come here. "I'm not really sure. It was a chance to be near my folks for a while. I needed—wanted," she amended quickly, "a change." Some of the places she'd shot this year had been depressing in the extreme. Perhaps she had needed the change, but she preferred to think of it as a choice rather than a need. "Anyway," she went on, "you've suggested some wonderful spots but I haven't found what I want yet."

"And what is that?"

She shrugged and gave him a helpless smile. "I won't know until I see it."

Justin nodded soberly, as though he understood. After a minute he spoke again, almost musingly. "Here in the islands, we walk a fine line between promoting tourism, which is important to our economy, and exploiting our resources." He sighed. "Occasionally we step over that line."

"Not often, thank goodness. That's one of the things that has impressed me as I've roamed around. The places I've seen are well-protected, but it is done without denying access to the people who want to share the beauty."

"Spoken like a true kamaaina."

Liz smiled at the appellation. She wasn't a native, of course. She didn't even fit the second definition of the Hawaiian word—a person who becomes a part of the islands and loves them as though they were home. To her these few weeks were a pleasant interlude, a stopover on her way to somewhere else. "Thanks."

Justin parked in a small parking lot, deserted at this time of night. She reached across the seat for her camera case and hopped out of the Jeep to join him on a path that led through the trees. The moonlight was bright as they made their way to the overlook.

As they drew closer, the thundering roar of the water plunging four hundred feet into a basin, which appeared much too small to contain such volume, drowned out other sounds. The display of raw power was overwhelming.

The moon rode just above the falls. The heady, exotic scent of wild ginger filled the air, turning the velvet night into a sensuous setting. Liz turned to Justin with a smile, her hands already busy with straps and her mind estimating light and filters. "This is a magical place. If I made three wishes here, they would probably come true." She had to raise her voice to be heard.

"Maybe. What would the wishes be?"

"I'd have to think about that. Thank you for bringing me," she said.

The moonlight painted her smiling features silver and turned her auburn hair black. Without thinking, Justin reached out to tuck a strand behind her ear. Her smile faded as his fingers brushed her cheek; the skin was warm and smooth. Uh-oh, thought Liz, remembering the effect of the kiss they had shared that afternoon. Careful.

As though he'd read her thoughts, he breathed deeply and stepped away. His voice was brisk as he said, "I'll hold your camera case." He slipped the wide strap from her shoulder. "God, this thing weighs a ton," he griped good-naturedly.

She laughed, disarmed by this side of him. When he grinned like that, revealing the elongated dimple in his cheek, when he teased her, which wasn't often, she was hard pressed to imagine any man more attractive. Every day he performed physical labor that would test a professional linebacker, so his complaint was absurd. So was her response—tenderness, inarguably. "That's why I have such strong muscles," she said.

She uncapped a lens and turned away. Her hands were steady, but only from effort, she noticed, uncomfortable with herself for being so easily affected. The first few shots would surely be wasted.

But soon her instincts began to take over. She raised the camera to her eyes and instantly she became the professional, moving quickly to experiment with angles, snapping and unsnapping filters as she went.

Justin stood propped comfortably with his back against a tree. Arms crossed, knee bent, one foot flattened on the tree, he watched, fascinated anew by this woman. Her movements were a fluid ballet of dip and pause, stretch and dip. Twice she returned to his side to exchange filters and once to replenish the film. He caught his breath when she moved onto a rock near the edge of the overhang.

The water had made the surface of the rock slick. But she was surefooted, even when the spray began to wet her clothes. He smiled—she had no fear for herself; all her concern was for her precious camera. Still he remained alert to her position, ready to haul her back if she got too close to trouble. Once she lowered the camera and swiped her face with her hand. When she stepped back, he breathed again.

Liz pivoted from the brink with an impatient step. The rock she stood on was too narrow to allow her to move freely; she'd try another spot. As she scanned the area, she wiped water off her face. The gesture dislodged one of her contacts, sending it flying. She muttered an expletive and dropped to her knee, hoping to catch a glimpse of the tiny thing.

Justin was there in an instant. "Liz! What happened? Damn it, you've got to be careful." As he spoke, his hands lifted her, crushing her into his strong arms and dragging her to level ground. "This rock is as slick as ice," he murmured roughly into her hair.

The camera was squeezed uncomfortably between them. "Ouch," said Liz.

"What is it? Are you hurt?" His arms loosened a fraction.

"Only where the camera lens is poking into my ribs," she said breathlessly, pulling it free. She looked at him and was surprised into silence. He was as white as a sheet. The arms that held her were shaking. "Justin, I'm okay," she said gently.

The sound of the falls drowned out her words, and his head blotted out the night. The kiss, brief as it was, was a mind-burning tornado compared to the one they'd shared that afternoon. His mouth consumed, claimed, insisted. He was breathing heavily when he broke off the kiss and touched her forehead with his. "You scared the hell out of me. Did you fall?"

Liz opened her eyes and tried to focus, but he was only a blur. "No. I lost my contact lens," she explained faintly. "And the other one isn't where it's supposed to be." Her head was reeling and her legs were weak from the powerful kiss. The displacement of one little old contact lens didn't surprise her at all. She wanted to draw away, to refit the remaining lens, but movement was beyond her. She felt very vulnerable.

"Contact lens? I didn't know you wore them."

She nodded. "And it will be the devil to find in this light."

"Okay. I've got a flashlight in the Jeep." He dropped his arm and she clutched at his shirt. "Wait. Don't leave me." She realized how wimpy her plea sounded, so she amended it. "I mean, let me get the other lens positioned so I can see. I don't want to walk off into the water."

"You mean you can't see at all without them?"

"Not much," she admitted with a nervous laugh. "And in this light, I'm blind as a bat."

He kept his hands at her waist as she bent her head forward. She held her eyelid open and blinked. The tears flowed freely and in a second the lens floated to its proper place. "There," she said, relieved.

"You'll be all right while I go for the flashlight?"

"I'll be fine."

Justin's long legs ate up the distance while his brain worried with his reaction to her helplessness. When she'd clutched at his shirt, it had been the first sign of anything approaching helplessness that Liz had ever shown, and he'd been surprised at the protective feelings that had sprung up, full-blown, in him.

When he got back, Liz was on her knees searching, but the moon didn't provide the right kind of illumination. He joined her and played the beam across the area she indicated.

"It's no use. The thing is so tiny, we'll never find it."

"Do you have a spare set?"

"No, just a pair of glasses, and they're back at the house." Finally she sat on her heels, scraped her long hair with the fingers of one hand and laughed without humor. "Maybe I should use one of my wishes."

"The moon would set before we could get to the house and back. Can't you work with one contact?" he asked.

She shot him a look. "Not very well," she said dryly. "If I'd just gotten a few more shots . . ."

"You might have to stay in Hawaii until the next full moon," said Justin casually, continuing to search. He was surprised at how much he wanted her to do just that. He caught a glimmer of something. . . . "Your first wish just came true. Here it is."

She leaned forward until their heads were almost touching. "Thank goodness. You must have eyes like an eagle, Justin. Give it to me."

"Liz, it's dirty. You can't put it into your eye like this."

"Oh, drat."

He took a handkerchief out of his hip pocket, carefully wrapped the tiny disk, and buttoned it in his breast pocket. Then he rose and held out his hand.

With one contact in place, she could easily see well enough to follow the path; she didn't need to hold on to his hand all the way back to the Jeep, but she did.

It was after midnight when they turned into the drive at Fairwinds. He left her at the door to her room. He didn't even try to kiss her.

Chapter Four

The next evening, Liz was late returning to Fair-
winds. Annie greeted her in the hall and explained that
Justin and Sondra had already gone upstairs to dress.
"Mrs. Hogan plans for you to have dinner at the
Kahlii Club. I believe she made the reservations for
seven-thirty."

Liz looked at her watch. "Oops, I'd better hurry.
Thanks, Annie."

She bathed quickly and dressed in another of her
trousseau gowns. This one was white crepe, and the
soft fabric draped demurely at her neck, leaving her
tanned arms bare, but the back plunged daringly to
her waist. She hesitated and added a gossamer white
stole before leaving the room.

In the upstairs hall she met Sondra, dressed in another of her colorful, floaty muumuus.

"What a lovely dress, Liz. Annie said she told you we are having dinner out tonight."

"I hope I haven't made you late. I went over to the village today to search for a developing lab. I met a fellow photographer who may be able to help me find a place. We got to talking and the time just slipped away."

"We're not late at all."

Standing below in the entrance hall, Justin watched them descend. He was an impressive sight in formal evening clothes. By the time Liz reached the bottom of the stairs, her knees were unsteady. She tried to tell herself the condition was a result of rushing, but his glittering green gaze wandering over her was a clear statement, as though she needed reminding, that he was finished with brotherly concern.

As they entered the club, Liz caught her breath at the dramatic sight that greeted her. The building was contemporary, perched on the side of a mountain, and the soaring glass walls gave a panoramic view of the countryside with sparkling lights below and twinkling stars above. "Oh, I wish I had my camera."

Justin chuckled. "High praise indeed," he said.

She grinned at him.

Sondra was also pleased at her reaction. "I thought you might enjoy seeing the view from here."

The maître d' approached. "Good evening, Mrs. Hogan. I have your table ready. If you'll follow me, please."

The round table was positioned in a corner of two glass walls. In the center of the white cloth, a floral arrangement mixed waxy red anthuriums with the broad, flat leaves of the ti plant. The table was set for seven. "This looks lovely, Charles," Sondra said as she settled into the chair the man was holding for her. "Liz, you sit there facing the view."

Justin pulled out Liz's chair, then inquired off-handedly, "Who's coming, Mother?"

"Babs is visiting her parents so I asked them to join us. Jay Stuart is escorting her. You don't mind, do you, dear?"

Liz, who had no idea who any of the people were, let her stole slip from her shoulders before she sat down. But she was fully aware of the sharp intake of breath behind her and wondered about it. "Thank you," she murmured politely, sneaking a look at Justin as he sat beside her. He was frowning. Was Babs something to him? She was surprised at her reaction. She found that she didn't want to meet this Babs person.

Her suspicions were confirmed when Sondra went on to explain. "The Simons are old friends. Their daughter, Babs Tremaine, was my daughter's age and spent a lot of time at our house. She is in the process of getting a divorce—very sad for all of them. They had a huge wedding only two years ago. It makes you wonder if young people today even try very hard." As she arranged her purse in her lap and straightened an already perfectly aligned spoon, she added too casually, "Justin and Babs had a thing at one time. But after the breakup, they remained friends." She turned to her son. "Didn't you, dear?"

"We were always friends, Mother." Justin's answer was bluntly delivered, but Liz had seen his reaction.

Without thinking, she laid her hand on his arm. She'd been through a breakup herself, as he well knew since he'd been a witness, and she couldn't imagine having to sit down to dinner with her ex-fiancé. He gave her an unreadable look.

"Here they are now," said Sondra.

Justin glanced over his shoulder. As he rose to greet the approaching foursome he muttered under his breath, "It promises to be a long night."

The guests had come to the table behind Liz. Rather than crane her neck around in unbecoming curiosity, she waited until they had exchanged their personal greetings.

Sondra directed the seating, then introduced Liz to John and Mildred Simon, who took chairs on the other side of Justin. They were quiet, prosperous-looking people who responded with friendly smiles.

In the chair to Liz's right, Jay Stuart gave the hovering waiter a drink order before he acknowledged the introduction and sat down. He had been blocking

Liz's line of sight, but as soon as he was seated, she got her first full look at Babs.

Liz became very still, engulfed by a grim and startling sense of déjà vu. Babs Tremaine, so that was the woman's name. She felt her heart settle somewhere near her toes, but except for a slight loss of color, her features remained fixed in the same polite expression.

Beneath the cover of the introductions and greetings she thought grimly that Justin was right; this would be a long night. A very long night.

Babs Tremaine's eyes roamed over her, dismissing her even as she mouthed the proper words in response to Sondra's introduction. She was the kind of woman around whom Liz had always felt inadequate, a beautiful woman, petite, with golden blonde curls and light blue eyes.

Suddenly those eyes returned to her face, narrowing suspiciously. Recognition flared.

Liz met the blue gaze with a cool one of her own.

Babs's gaze was the first to falter. She fingered the round neckline of her yellow silk dress. Then she leaned forward to smile beguilingly—over Jay and Liz—at Justin. "It's so good to be home, Justin. Tell me, what's been going on? Have you seen any of the old crowd?" Jay joined in and they went on to discuss people unknown to Liz. She tuned them out and dealt instead with the churning emotions inside her.

The waiter, who had been making his way around the table, reached her side.

Liz hesitated, then ordered a gin and tonic. When it came she drank thirstily and tried to pretend interest in the beautiful decor of the club. The menus were presented; she took a long time to study hers.

With Sondra as a sounding board, and without being intentionally rude, the older couple picked up the personal small talk of people who have known each other for a long time. Babs's vivacious chatter grew in direct proportion to Liz's silence. Pretty, diminutive Babs, apart from the antipathy that flared between them, made Liz feel clumsy and awkward in comparison. It was a miserable situation.

To add to her discomfort, Justin was giving her frequent suspicious glances. When the waiter returned to take their orders for dinner, he used the distraction to lean closer and murmur in an undertone, "You're wearing that look again."

"What look?" she asked stiffly.

"That same look you wore the first time I met you. Like you're bored stiff. What's the matter?"

Liz almost laughed but at the last minute she managed to bite off the laughter, which, she knew, would have come out sounding hysterical. If only she could escape from here, play sick or something. "Please, Justin, don't make the same mistake you made then. You wouldn't understand."

"Try me."

"No," she said flatly. "It's a personal matter that I don't wish to discuss." She wasn't about to admit to this man that the Shirley Temple doll seated across the table was her own personal nemesis—had, in fact, caused the breakup of her engagement.

Liz railed against a fate that had thrown her together with this woman. But wasn't that why she'd left the islands a year ago? Because many members of the military community, including her own parents, frequently socialized with prominent civilians. She had no idea where Taylor had met the woman, but she had feared an encounter just like this one. So she had left.

"Have it your way," Justin said dismissively. His face took on another degree of sternness.

Sondra had explained that Liz was photographing the island for the Visitors' Bureau. When Jay spoke to her, asking about her job, she turned to answer him with a feeling akin to relief.

It was clear after the first few minutes that Jay was jealous of Justin. She wondered if Justin was jealous of him, as well. After all, Jay was here as Babs's escort—Babs was a busy lady, Liz thought wryly. Sondra had revealed that Babs and Justin had "a thing." So why had Babs married someone else?

And, the bigger question, if Babs was married at the time, what was she doing in bed with her—Liz's—fiancé a year ago?

Finally their dinner was served. Liz ate what was placed in front of her without tasting a bite. Jay kept up a conversation, for which she was grateful because in his condition, it didn't much matter whether her responses made sense or not. He had consumed two drinks to everyone else's one, and the more he drank, the more interest he seemed to take in her, but his questions were trivial and his attention was easily diverted.

During dinner a combo had begun to play for dancing, and as soon as the table was cleared Jay started to speak. But Justin got in first. "Would you like to dance, Liz?" he asked.

Since he clearly was in a disapproving mood, she was surprised that he hadn't asked the little blonde instead. Perhaps his pride wouldn't let him. She didn't know the circumstances of their breakup, and she couldn't imagine any woman preferring another man over Justin. If Babs had hurt him deeply, though, he wouldn't give her a chance to repeat. Liz had learned enough about him to be sure of that.

"Thank you," she answered, relieved to get away from the table, if only for a few minutes. "I'd love to dance." She rose to lead the way to the dance floor.

As Justin's large hand made contact with her bare back, Liz went rigid with a sudden shock of electricity that flooded her senses. Unable to disguise her reaction, her wide eyes flew to his. Her cheeks were burning. "Justin . . ." Her voice was a thin thread of sound.

"Yeah. It's pretty shocking, isn't it? But where else does a man put his hand if he wants to dance with you?" His fingers moved slowly over her skin.

The smooth caress fueled the flame. Their bodies brushed lightly, adding sparks. Mutual awareness riveted their gazes. Finally Liz lowered her eyes. "Please," she whispered.

He tightened his arm, shifting his hand to her hip, and brought her closer to his hard thighs. "Is that better?"

Her knees almost gave way completely. "Stop it," she commanded.

"You can bet Jay is anticipating his first dance with you. He's been eyeing the back of your dress all during dinner. You'd better watch your step with him, Liz. He has quite a reputation, and the innocent act won't matter at all."

Act? Did he think it was an act? She felt her disappointment build. She'd thought he understood. She tried to keep her voice light. "There you go again," she admonished, shaking her head.

"What are you talking about?"

"That warning was deserving of my brother at his most protective. I am old enough and perfectly capable of taking care of myself, thank you."

His green eyes grew dark, like a storm over the Atlantic. "Now you *are* playing with fire. You ought to know by now how I feel about being compared to brother James."

The music ended; she pulled out of his arms and turned to go back to the table. He held her chair, but, before sitting down, she picked up the soft white stole she had draped over the back. Placing it around her shoulders, she knotted the ends loosely across her breasts.

"Chilly?" inquired Justin with a raised brow. But he visibly relaxed, and there was a hint of laughter in his eyes as they met hers.

Her lips twitched in response but she denied him mutual amusement. "A little bit," she answered calmly.

Later, when Jay asked her to dance, Justin stood up with Babs. Jay took Liz in his arms; she felt nothing. But when she watched Justin's arm encircle Babs's tiny waist, watched him lean down to hear something Babs was saying, she felt a pang of regret.

Liz excused herself after the dance was finished and headed for the powder room. She sank onto a padded stool in front of the mirror and plucked a tissue from the box on the narrow shelf.

Sondra came in almost immediately. "What do you think of Babs?" she asked as she tucked in a stray strand of hair.

Liz hid her eyes in the search for a lipstick from her bag. "She's lovely."

Sondra sighed dramatically. "Yes, lovely but careless, I'm afraid."

Despite her better judgment, Liz was curious. "Careless?" she asked.

"She has barely spoken to poor Jay tonight. He's been in love with her since they were children. My daughter had a crush on Jay for a while, but he couldn't see her for Babs, who always seemed to prefer Justin, but then married that Tremaine man from Honolulu."

Liz gave a chuckle. "I'm afraid this is all too complicated for me."

Sondra agreed. "It sounds like a soap opera, doesn't it? I think Babs has decided she wants Justin again, but I can't imagine his taking her back when she let him down once, can you?"

"I don't know him well enough to judge, Sondra. If he really loves her..."

"Bosh. I doubt that he ever did. It was a case of wishful thinking on our part."

But Liz wasn't sure. She remembered the catch in Justin's voice when he'd heard that Babs would be joining them. "It looks to be a long night," he'd said. At that moment, the subject of their conversation pushed open the swinging door to enter the room.

Sondra's expression changed from that of concerned parent to gracious hostess. "Babs, my dear, I'm so glad you could join us tonight. When are you returning to Honolulu, or are you home to stay?"

Babs looked surprised; then she tittered—she actually tittered! For the first time Liz studied Babs with a professional eye rather than a personal one. Pretty, no doubt about that, with a skin-deep, surface beauty, not much more. She could understand Sondra's use of the word careless. But, she noticed suddenly, there was something else...a look of unhappiness, perhaps. Her camera could find those deeper feelings, perhaps explain them.

Babs's gaze flickered to Liz, catching the study.

Liz immediately felt the sting in that blue gaze.

Babs turned away. "I've lived so long in Honolulu, I almost think of that as home. But I'm not sure how long I'll be here. It depends, Sondra, on a lot of things."

"Oh?" The older woman raised an inquiring brow. Liz was struck by the marked resemblance to her son in the peculiarity.

Babs didn't answer the unspoken question. Instead she turned to Liz. "How long will you be in the islands, Miss Ennis?"

It was the first time she had spoken directly to Liz since they were introduced a couple of hours ago. Liz felt moisture in her palms. She was saved from having to answer by Sondra.

"Call her Liz, Babs. She's only been here a short time but she's become like a member of the family."

Babs's eyes narrowed. "Really? How nice for her. How long will you be here, Liz?"

Liz's wayward tongue answered before she took time to think. In a parody of Babs's earlier statement, she answered sweetly, "That depends, Babs, on a lot of things." With the words she tilted her chin and met the eyes of the blonde in the mirror.

Sondra laughed triumphantly.

Babs was disconcerted by the reply. She muttered something, turned and quickly left the room.

Sondra made no further comment on the exchange, but there was a gleam in her eye and a satisfied smile on her lips.

Finally the evening, which had seemed endless, drew to a close. The party waited on the broad steps of the club for the cars to be brought around. Liz had managed to avoid any other conversational contact, except of the most general kind, with Babs. But while they stood there, Babs turned to her with a peculiar smile.

Liz felt her heart sink with the question: "Why is the name Ennis so familiar to me?" *Leave it,* she wanted to say. Instead she smiled and shrugged noncommittally.

"Liz's father is the commanding officer at the Naval Air Station at Barber's Point on Oahu," Sondra offered. And Liz's heart took another plunge.

"Oh, of course. We have mutual friends," Babs went on with a pretense at friendliness, but there was pure malice in her gaze. "At least one," she added.

She was about to add something else when Liz turned to glare at her. "Who should remain nameless, don't you think? Unless you'd prefer to start some rather ugly gossip?" she suggested. Her tone was blunt, almost rude, and clearly a warning to Babs to shut her mouth.

Silence descended. Liz regretted the outburst; it had been much more harsh than she'd intended. Sondra was bound to be curious now. But to her mind she'd had no choice. The whole evening had been tension-filled and uncomfortable. She wasn't about to get into a battle of semantics with this woman now that the end was in sight. And she wasn't willing to balance on the edge of innuendo and suggestion any longer.

Babs's eyes widened ingenuously. She looked from Liz to Justin, who wore a grim look, and spoke with studied confusion and fake embarrassment. "I'm sorry. I didn't mean to—"

Justin broke into her statement. He shot Liz a chastising look, then his expression shuttered. "Here's your car," he said abruptly to Babs. The parking attendant drove under the porte cochere and hopped out to head back to the lot. Justin stepped off the curb and opened the back door for Babs and the front for her mother. Babs lingered for a last word. Her hand rested possessively on Justin's sleeve. He said something under his breath, which provoked a lilting laugh from Babs.

There were other undercurrents here besides her own, Liz decided. Jay, who had sobered while they were dancing, had been silent during the exchange. Now, with his eyes averted from the couple, he murmured his thanks to Sondra and rounded the car on unsteady legs. The proper and polite goodbyes were exchanged. Mr. Simon took the wheel and the car moved off down the long driveway.

Liz schooled herself not to let out an audible sigh of relief. When Justin's car arrived, she climbed into the back seat and sank into the plush cushions.

Sondra half turned in her seat. She talked, jabbered really, throughout the ride to Fairwinds. It occurred to Liz that Sondra had recognized her distress and was giving her a chance to recover.

Only she knew how difficult that was going to prove. She slid a glance to Justin's forbidding profile. This evening, the blonde had very effectively reinforced his opinion of her as the spoiled admiral's daughter. She tried to tell herself she was being unreasonable. Justin had known Babs for years. Certainly he would resent anyone snapping at her as Liz had done.

She certainly had no claims to his allegiance. Even though there were strong emotions brewing between them, a few days of knowing her was nothing compared to a lifetime of friendship—or more. Liz stared blindly out the window for the rest of the drive, responding to Sondra's chatter only when it was necessary.

After Justin had bid a terse good-night to his mother, he caught Liz's arm in a light grip. "Have a nightcap with me?"

Though it was phrased as a question, she had no doubt that he wouldn't be pleased—to say the least— if she refused. There was a glint in his eyes that she didn't quite trust. But she agreed to the nightcap, finally facing the idea that his thinking ill of her hurt more than she would admit. Maybe she could smooth things over.

"Sherry, right?" he asked when they reached his study.

Liz nodded, then realizing his back was to her, answered in a soft voice. "Please." She sank onto the leather sofa where they had spent so many pleasant hours planning her itinerary. She wondered if this conversation would mark an end to the feelings that had developed between them.

Justin handed her the stemmed glass and crossed the room to stand staring down at his desk. He turned on his desk lamp and extinguished the overhead light, plunging the room into a shadowy darkness, lit only by the sharply defined pool of light on the surface of the desk. As a result, his expression was barely visible as he joined her on the sofa.

They spoke together.

"Justin . . ."

"Liz . . ."

He indicated that she should go first.

She sat up straighter and said, like a child reciting a lesson, "Justin, I would like to apologize for snapping at your guest."

His lips curved in a small smile—or she thought it was a smile. "Did she deserve it?"

Liz was surprised by the question. "Well, yes, she did," she answered honestly.

Justin sighed. "I was afraid of that. Babs is a bit spoiled—we've all spoiled her. As a child she suffered through a long illness. It's no excuse, but it might be a reason for her rather single-minded approach to what she wants."

"And she wants you," Liz supplied.

"Not really. She may think she does," he said off-handedly.

He didn't sound like a broken-hearted suitor. So she asked the question that had puzzled her all evening. "Now you can answer something for me. All evening you acted like a bear with a thorn in its paw. Why?"

From his expression, she knew he hadn't expected that. "I told you why," he answered reluctantly. "When we were dancing."

Liz thought, but she couldn't remember anything significant they'd said. All she could recall was the feel of his arms around her, his hand on her bare skin. "You mean my dress?" she said, flabbergasted.

"Yes, I mean your dress," he growled. "The thing is close to being indecent."

Liz touched her finger to her lips thoughtfully. Her eyes, half hidden by her long lashes, slid to his. "You're pretty conservative for a smooth-talking bachelor."

His eyes narrowed. "And I thought you weren't good at games." When she laughed, deep in her throat, he started to reach for her.

She held him off with her hand. "Sorry," she said hastily.

He settled back and took a swallow from his glass. "There were things left unsaid between the two of you tonight, weren't there?"

She didn't have to ask who he was talking about. They were back to Babs again. And there was no point in denying his assumption when she'd practically told Babs to shut up in front of everybody. "Yes."

"Babs intimated as much."

Liz's head swung around to him. Another surprise. "She did?" She couldn't imagine Babs telling Justin the truth, that she'd been unfaithful to her husband—and with Liz's fiancé. "What did she say?" Her hand shook slightly as she placed her glass on the coffee table before them.

Justin drank from his glass and set it beside hers. His green eyes were hooded. "She said she was a friend of your ex-fiancé. She suggested that you might have broken your engagement, deciding I would be a better catch."

Liz inhaled sharply; her hands made fists. "That's ridiculous. I hadn't even met you then."

"Babs didn't know that."

The little witch! But, in a way, Liz was glad. For some reason it was unthinkable that this man should be witness to her humiliation—any more than he already was. She forced her fingers open. "But I could have known who you were. Tell me, did you swallow her suggestion?" she asked evenly.

He chuckled softly. "If I hadn't been a witness to your pain that night a year ago, I might have. But, no, I didn't. However," he went on, "I want to know the reason for the animosity between you."

He wasn't going to give up. She sighed. "That's too bad, because I have no intention of telling you."

"Maybe Babs will."

If the statement was a threat, it was a flawed one. She couldn't imagine the blonde confessing infidelity, not to him of all people. Of course, he couldn't know that. "Ask her," said Liz as she rose. "Thanks for the nightcap, Justin. Good night."

He was up in an instant and had her by the arm. He swung her around until they were touching. "Babs's husband has a roving eye. Did it settle on you?"

It was the last thing she expected to hear, but if she laughed now, she would never stop. "Now that's insulting, Justin," she said. "Don't you and your girlfriend have anything more interesting to speculate about?"

Justin was clearly annoyed by the accusation. "She is not my girlfriend," he said firmly. "But, despite her faults, she is a good friend."

When she gave him a dubious look he added, "Hell, Liz, Babs is still married."

"Not so much that you would notice," she said spitefully.

His gaze became hooded. The heat from his body was like a threat to her good intentions. "What do you mean by that?"

"Let go of me."

Instead of complying, he slid his hand around her nape. "I don't think so." His mouth came down to cover hers in a slow, potent, thorough kiss. She made herself stand rigid and unresponsive.

He raised his head and looked deeply into her eyes. At last he released her. "Go to bed, Liz," he said roughly, picking up his glass again.

"Justin—"

He looked at her over the rim of his glass. "Unless you're ready to answer my questions, I suggest you go to bed."

She left without another word.

Liz's head rolled on the pillow and she stared blindly at the ceiling, wondering at the whims of providence. How could one person cause such havoc in another person's life? She tried not to think but her memory was insistent, picking at her, forcing her to recall the afternoon a year ago....

Liz had never known, never cared to know, the woman's name. She had arrived early for her date with Taylor. She was no more than ten feet away when the door of his apartment opened. The image that remained seared on her brain was distinct—her fiancé was saying a passionate goodbye to another woman, warm and mussed from what was unmistakably an afternoon of lovemaking. His hand rested familiarly on the lovely young woman's derriere as they said their soft goodbyes and exchanged a last kiss.

Liz stood there in the hot sunlight, stunned into immobility, unable to tear her eyes from the couple. Surely she was dreaming, surely she would awaken in a minute.

They must have felt the sudden tension in the atmosphere, or maybe she made a sound, for they turned to look at her. For uncounted seconds the three of them were a frozen tableau. "My God," Taylor cried at last, his expression almost comical. His arms dropped and he took a step toward Liz.

At his movement, she knew suddenly that this was no dream. She turned to flee. Before she reached her car, he caught up with her, grasping her arm. "Liz, listen to me. This isn't what it looks like."

Silently she raised her burning eyes to his, then she shifted her gaze to the woman who stood watching them, a small smile on her doll-like face.

"It was just..." He groped for an explanation, sounding desperate. "A last fling, you know."

Liz was still focused on the woman and she saw the effect of his words. The blonde's face fell like that of a child whose favorite toy has been broken. The sight provoked a brief but unexpectedly sympathetic reaction in Liz, surprising her. But her sympathy faded almost instantly as he gave her arm a shake. Her gaze returned to him. His face was as white as the blouse she wore. "Liz!" he said again.

She was filled with loathing and revulsion. The pain would come later, she was sure, but for now, her only need was to escape his presence. "Take your hand off me," she told him. They were the first words she'd spoken and she was pleased at how controlled she sounded. She had pronounced each word distinctly.

Stung by her constraint, he dropped his hand. She turned away to get into her car.

That was her first encounter with Babs Tremaine and her last glimpse of the man she'd been about to marry. It was a further irony that a short while later she would have her first encounter with Justin Hogan.

She kicked off the sheets. Though she had been rocked severely tonight by the appearance of Babs, there was no pain in remembering the scene with her fiancé. The only pain she felt was in having Justin know that she had been betrayed for a woman he cared about. Call it pride, call it vanity, she didn't want him to find out.

Chapter Five

For the next several days Liz plunged into her work and timed her hours at the house in order to avoid Justin. She knew he would press for explanations, and she had no intention of explaining to him why she despised his "good friend."

Evading him was not too difficult. She'd never known a man to work so hard. He was usually gone by the time she got out of bed in the mornings, and she had found a film processing company in Hilo willing to let her use their facilities after business hours, when he would return to the house for dinner.

One really good thing arose from the situation. She began to make significant progress on the assignment. Liz was her own worst critic, but most of the work she had done was good, very good. Some of it was exceptional. With all she had on her mind—unexpectedly meeting her nemesis, Babs Tremaine, on the heels of her overwhelming awareness of Justin Hogan, and his friendship with the woman—the quality of the photos surprised and pleased her.

Maybe she could get this job over quickly and get away from here before Justin became any more damaging to her peace of mind. The pressure built a bit more every time she was around him. So she rose early and stayed away from the house for as long as possible.

She tried to tell herself that she didn't miss the evenings spent in his study, curled up on the soft leather sofa, talking over the day just past and making plans for the next one. But the truth was, she did miss them. She missed him too much.

From snippets of information that Sondra let drop, she was learning a lot about him. The more she learned, the more she admired the man for his sense of responsibility. That was a characteristic he shared with her father.

Justin had been nineteen, in school back east, when his father died. Sondra always passed over that part quickly, as though she couldn't bear to talk about her husband's death. Justin had quit school and come home. From then until now, she gathered, he'd devoted himself to the ranch, forswearing travel, except for business trips, and vacations. From what Sondra added, he wasn't much for socializing, either.

If Liz had thought Justin wouldn't notice her deliberate absences, she was sadly mistaken. He noticed all right, and grew more taciturn each time they did happen to meet. A simple greeting could earn her a short reply.

One night, it was after eleven when she returned to the house after working through dinner at the processing lab. Her grumbling stomach reminded her that she hadn't eaten and she decided to raid the refrigerator. She was juggling a platter of ham, a jar of mustard and a ripe, red tomato, when he came up on cat feet behind her.

"Can I help you find something?" he asked mildly, startling her out of her skin.

"Drat!" She managed to hold on to the platter of ham, he caught the mustard, but the ripe tomato hit the floor with a splat. "Don't sneak up on me like that!" she ordered, setting the platter on the counter with a definite thump. Her hands were shaking; she grabbed for a paper towel from the roll and started to clean up the mess.

But the towel didn't tear where it was supposed to, she slipped in tomato juice, and before she knew it she was tangled in towels.

"I wasn't sneaking around," said Justin, trying unsuccessfully to muffle his laughter. "I live here." He separated the paper towel from the roll and her from the floor with a single smooth gesture.

"Sorry," she muttered.

He directed her to sit at the table while he wiped tomato pulp from the floor and wall. By the time he finished, she had regained her composure. He opened the refrigerator and took out another tomato. He also collected plates, a knife and a loaf of bread. "I'm hungry, too. Do you like pickles on your sandwich?"

She picked up the tomato and the knife. "Yes, please."

"Dill or sweet?"

"Dill," she said sourly.

He got the pickles from the cabinet. "Shall I make coffee?"

"I'd better have milk," said Liz.

Justin arched a brow. "Trouble sleeping? I could warm it for you," he said easily.

She met his amused gaze and relented; laughing, she answered, "No, thank you. Cold will be fine."

She finished with the tomato and began to work on the ham. He was spreading mustard on the sliced bread. She watched from the corner of her eye, her gaze on his large, strong hands. He worked deftly, surprising her. He was quite at home in the kitchen. She would have been willing to wager that this man never prepared food for himself. And she would have been wrong.

Justin watched from the corner of his eye as Liz sliced the tomato. She had lovely hands. Her nails were not exaggeratedly long but were well cared for. Her fingers were slim and capable.

For several minutes they worked together, comfortably but without conversation.

Justin had learned very little about this woman, and the more he learned, the less he seemed to know. She was a puzzle, and he'd always been intrigued by puzzles.

When she had explained the reasons for her cold manner the night they'd met—the first time—he'd immediately squelched his view of her as a spoiled brat. Instead, he admired the strength it took to walk into a room full of people after what she'd been through.

He genuinely regretted misjudging her, but then another puzzling thing had happened at the club. She had reacted to Babs as though his friend were a leper. He couldn't understand Liz's reaction, and she refused to discuss it. But he would figure it out. Or ask Babs.

Babs was a lovable scatterbrain but she wasn't hateful—as far as he knew, and he'd known her all her life. Once he'd entertained thoughts—and that was all they were, thoughts—of marriage to Babs. At that time she, too, had been a bird with bright feathers, a vagabond, ready to fly off to the next adventure. Just like Liz. But he knew such a marriage wouldn't work. When she had announced that she was marrying someone else, he'd wondered why he wasn't more upset.

He hadn't been tempted to marry since. He hadn't written off the possibility, someday, if he found the right woman. But more likely, he was destined to be the crotchety uncle of his sister's kids—if she and her husband ever decided to have any—who stayed on the island and took care of the business. If the life was occasionally lonely, he could handle it. There were plenty of women who were more than willing to help him deal with loneliness on a temporary basis, and he took the safe path with them. They knew the score going in. They knew he wasn't going to become emotionally involved or care too much.

He was intelligent enough to speculate that perhaps his iron-clad control over his feelings was a form of self-protection, but there was nothing wrong with that. He didn't admire the modern tendency to regurgitate one's confidences all over someone else. If that put him beyond the pale as a modern man, so be it.

Liz Ennis wasn't the type to settle for the rancher's life-style that was mandatory for him, any more than Babs had been. Not many women were the type. Even his mother, who had been content here for thirty-five years, had recently been showing signs of restlessness. She traveled more these days, mostly to California where his sister lived, in hopes of convincing Jeanne to start a family. He grinned, picturing the debate.

Liz had been quiet for a long time. He realized suddenly that the silence in the room had stretched out too long, to a tension-filled point. He didn't want that to happen. He had come looking for Liz tonight. He'd missed her company; he wanted to have a quiet hour with her, to talk.

The sandwiches were ready and he'd grabbed a sack of potato chips. They sat at the table in the bay window. After a bite or two he asked, "Tell me how you got started in photography."

That was a nice safe subject, Liz decided. "It was love at first click," she said. "For my fourteenth birthday, Daddy gave me my first real camera."

Justin grinned, activating that sexy slash in his tanned cheek. "A real camera? As opposed to an unreal one?" He crunched his strong, white teeth on a potato chip and waited for an explanation.

Liz had to make a determined effort to look away from his well-shaped mouth. *See,* she told herself, *you were wise to avoid this man as much as possible.* "As opposed to a 'point and shoot,'" she explained. "That camera was gloriously complicated, with f-stops and filters, light meter and changeable lenses and everything. I've been taking pictures ever since. My poor mother has them all. Thousands of them. Someday the navy is bound to question why the weight of their household goods is so high when they have to move."

"How did you get started professionally? You freelance and yet you're young to be so successful." He wanted to keep her talking. The house was quiet, everyone else was asleep, and he was enjoying the feeling of intimacy, of being the only two people awake. If she stopped talking, she would leave him and go to bed.

He thought again that she was one of the sexiest women he'd ever met. Her long legs, her full breasts, the way she moved, her gestures—so graceful for a tall woman and so assured—aroused and excited him. He also appreciated the fact that they fit together well; he didn't have to break his back to dance with her.

He recalled the morning she had accused him of sounding like her brother. He hadn't relished the comparison, and that had surprised him, considering that was exactly how he'd been treating her. What did he want from her? he asked himself.

After the kiss they'd shared in the swimming pool, after the impassioned way she responded to him, he'd thought her... reluctant, but just possibly persuadable, if he handled her very carefully. The only other question lay with him, with his motives. He hadn't answered that one yet. He simply knew that he liked to be with her.

Liz took another bite of her sandwich and chewed. She touched her napkin to her mouth before she answered his last question. "Sorry, I was starving." She took a swallow of milk. "I didn't start out freelancing. I went to college, but that didn't last more than a year. I knew what I wanted to do and they didn't teach it in school. So I quit to work with a man in New York, who accepted a few students—interns, really—each year."

She mentioned the name of a well-known photographer. Justin was further impressed. "I hated my first job, but it paid the bills," she went on.

He was distracted for a moment by another perspective of her, reflected on the windowpanes. Beyond the windows the night was pitch black.

"I took pictures of those gimmicky items in cheap catalogs. I've always disliked studio work and this was worse than most." She looked over at him with a frown. "Can you imagine trying to make designer toothbrushes look appealing, or setting up a shot of a toilet seat cover that plays Christmas carols?"

Justin laughed, thoroughly enjoying the tale. His sandwich lay forgotten on his plate. He folded his arms on the table and leaned forward. "How did you get yourself out of that?" he asked, admiring the play of light on her hair.

"I heard about a job that was opening up in one of the nature magazines. I applied and was accepted, mostly because of a glowing recommendation from the catalog editor. He'd never had anyone who did so well with singing toilet seat covers."

Liz had been speaking between bites and now she looked across the table at him and grinned. He grinned back and noticed that she'd finished eating. "Do you want something else? Annie made a chocolate cake for dessert tonight. It was good."

"No, thank you." She patted her stomach. "I couldn't eat another bite." She raised her hands to push back her hair and completed the action by lifting her arms to stretch. "I'm pooped. If my legs will take me upstairs, I'm going to bed."

None of her movements was deliberately provocative but, watching the thrust of her breasts against her shirt, Justin felt as if he'd been punched in the gut and dropped into hot oil at the same time. He was stunned by the desire that threatened to overwhelm his control. He didn't like it worth a damn. Unconsciously, he sought a way to get back at her for something that was no fault of hers.

"There's just one thing I don't understand about you," he said, trying to banish the throbbing in the lower part of his body. The statement came out with too much force. What the hell was he doing?

Liz swallowed a yawn and dropped her hands to her lap. She had slowly relaxed in his presence; but, with his abrupt remark, tension once again replaced the casual atmosphere. She wasn't sure why. "What's that?" she asked warily.

"I don't understand why you dislike Babs Tremaine, when you don't even know her."

Liz shrugged but her heart took a tumble. She started to gather up the plates and crumpled napkins. It seemed that every time she began to feel comfortable around this man he turned and snapped at her like a bad-tempered dog. *We were both enjoying this. Why did you have to spoil it?* she thought sadly.

"And why do you refuse to discuss her?"

Her voice was even and she was proud that her temper didn't swing totally out of control; but for her own sake she had to put an end to his curious speculation. Now. "That woman—"

His brows joined in a forbidding frown. "Her name is Babs," he interrupted sharply. "Why can't you be courteous enough to use it?"

With that, her temper did burst free. She stood up, scraping her chair noisily across the floor. "She is your friend and your mother's. I don't like to be rude when I'm a guest in your home so, as I see it, I have two choices. I can leave, or I can stay. If we are thrown together, I will be as polite to her as she is to me."

She planted her palms on the table and leaned forward for emphasis, her eyes sparking angrily. "You can decide and let me know which it is to be. But I want to tell you something, Justin Hogan. Whether you understand my reasons or not, I don't give a happy damn about that woman. And, if I am to stay, I'd appreciate it if you'd show me some of the same courtesy and get off my case about her."

She straightened, grabbed her camera case from where she'd left it on the counter and started to leave the kitchen. She stopped at the door to glare at him. "You can do the dishes," she said.

Justin stared, jaw slightly agape, at the empty door until her footsteps faded completely. He shook his head and whistled softly. He crossed his arms over his chest and tilted his chair against the wall. Slowly a smile spread across his face. Well, well, well. So, she did have a redheaded temper and she was glorious when she erupted. He began to chuckle. He didn't give a hoot whether she and Babs got along or not. But he was sure of something. He wasn't going to let her get away from him.

Here, he amended—he wasn't going to let her get away from *here*. Not anytime soon. She was far too interesting to have around.

On Saturday as Liz was leaving the house, Sondra stopped her in the hall. "Guess who I spoke with last night?" she asked brightly. Then she went on without waiting for an answer, which Liz couldn't have given anyway. "Your mother."

"My mother?" She had a terrible thought. "Has something happened?"

"No, no. I didn't mean to alarm you, Liz. I called to invite them to come to Fairwinds for the weekend. Unfortunately they can't stay, but they are coming to the party tonight. Imagine," she added in wonder. "They are going to fly down."

Her father would rent a plane, of course. He loved to fly. It wasn't unusual for him and her mother to hop on a plane and fly somewhere for dinner.

Liz had forgotten the party. "It was nice of you to invite them, Sondra. When are they coming? Shall I pick them up?"

Sondra waved her hand. "Not necessary. I've made arrangements for one of the men to meet them at the airport." She cocked her head and gave Liz a measured look. "You've been pushing hard, so get home in time to rest before the party."

Liz grinned, with an effort. "Do I look haggard?" she asked.

"Of course not. But I don't want your parents to think we've been mistreating you."

Liz knew what she looked like, especially after the fit she threw last night. The circles under her eyes were dark and the frown line between her brows was pronounced. "I've got to finish this assignment fairly soon. I have other things—" She broke off.

"Has Justin offended you in some way, Liz?" Sondra asked quietly.

Liz's eyes widened. "No, of course not."

"Well, he's my son and I love him, but I can also see his faults. I'm afraid that my husband's untimely death put too much responsibility on Justin at too early an age. He's a bit of a tyrant sometimes, just like his father was." She sighed. "If he'd married, he might have mellowed some—but I told you that story, didn't I?"

Oh, yes, she'd heard that story. "Yes, you did."

"If Justin is bothering you, just tell me and I'll keep him away."

He bothered her all right, but not in the way that Sondra intimated. "That isn't necessary," said Liz. Her voice was just a degree cooler. "I can handle it, thank you, Sondra."

"Good. I thought you would say that." Sondra was clearly pleased by Liz's response. "Have a nice day, dear."

Liz almost choked on a laugh. Mentally she shook herself, and left by the front door.

She drove south around the curve of the island to the Black Sand Beaches. It was a long drive, an hour and a half, giving her plenty of time to think. Her father and mother were coming. She'd be glad to see them, but she was also wary of what they might see in her.

Later, as she wandered the beach, her thoughts kept returning to Justin. She knelt and scooped some of the dark glistening sand—really pulverized grains of the lava from which these islands were formed. The grains trickled through her fingers as she gazed out over the sapphire waters of the Pacific. But she didn't see the ocean. Instead a rugged, sun-tanned face with glittering green eyes appeared before her. She was hypnotized by the image, and her body remembered the touch of his hands, the strength of his arms. She moistened her lips, recalling his taste.

What on earth was wrong with her? She'd never been so physically aroused by a man, not even her fiancé. She stood abruptly, dusted her hands and headed to the car, her camera case unopened. She gave up all pretense of work and began the long drive to Fairwinds.

Maybe Sondra would need help in preparing for the party.

When she reached the house and entered the large hall, she recognized that for the excuse it was. Everything, as usual, was spotless and shining, enticing aromas wafted from the direction of the kitchen, and fresh flowers abounded. She followed her nose, looking for Annie but, upon entering the kitchen, she found Sondra instead. The older woman made a striking picture, surrounded by pails of water filled with exotic blooms. She was putting finishing touches on two flower arrangements.

"Liz! You *are* back early. I'm glad."

"I decided to take your suggestion and rest for a while before the party. What time do the admiral and his lady arrive?"

"At seven. We'll have cocktails on the lanai and dinner about eight."

"Sounds great. I'll be down before seven."

Liz had arranged her hair on top of her head, letting a few tendrils escape to curl on her nape. She had decided to wear a turquoise silk *holomuu*, the dress favored by Polynesian dancers because of the way it defined the body. The off-the-shoulder gown molded her curves to a point at the knee. There, it flared into a floor-length flounce, slightly longer in the back.

She told herself that she wasn't competing with Babs, but she wanted something dramatic, something that Babs couldn't have worn. And this dress was dramatic, exactly matching her eyes.

It was going to be even more dramatic, she thought wryly, if she couldn't get it zipped and hooked. Sondra's footsteps had passed her door a short while ago, and she wished she'd known then how difficult the dress was to fasten.

It was almost seven o'clock. She had slept for a full hour, but she was unaccustomed to napping and had awakened with a sleep hangover that left her groggy and uncoordinated. Finally, in frustration, she rang for Annie and sat down on the chaise longue to wait.

She was looking forward to being with her parents for a few hours. Since reaching adulthood, she had developed a strong streak of independence, but tonight Babs would be here. She needed the anchor, the mooring, that their presence would provide.

When the knock came, she was surprised at the promptness of the response.

"Come in, Annie," she called as she rose, ready with her request. "I can't get—"

It wasn't Annie who entered, but Justin. In his hands was a long white carnation lei. At the sight of him her heart began its now familiar race with her breathing. He was not the man for her, she kept reminding herself, but just being in the same room with him could dissolve her resolution like a wisp of cloud before the wind. The top button of his tuxedo shirt was open, and his black tie dangled. He looked tired, too, she noticed.

Without taking his eyes off her, he closed the door behind him. His expression was hard to read as his eyes explored her leisurely, lingering longest on the curve of her breast above the dress she clutched in front of her. His eyes darkened dangerously.

Suddenly the room seemed to lift itself into an-other dimension, became foreign territory. Move-ment was suspended and Liz could only stare. Everything about the moment was otherworldly and strange. She had to resist the temptation to back off.

Finally, she forced inconsequential words past the lump in her throat. "I thought you were Annie. I can't get my dress fastened." Her voice seemed to come from far, far away.

Justin blinked as though awakening from a trance. She didn't realize he'd been leaning against the door until he levered himself away and approached her in what appeared to be slow motion. He held the flowered garland out and said, "This is for you. An apology for last night. And I hope you'll stay as long as possible."

Liz automatically put out her hand and he looped the lei over her wrist. "There's no need for an apol-ogy. It is I who should apologize, for losing my tem-per." Her eyes fell and she touched the fresh flowers. "Thank you. The lei is beautiful."

When he didn't reply she looked at him again. "Liz…" He took the lei from her nerveless fingers and tossed it on the dressing table. His hands were firm on her bare shoulders. His green eyes searched hers, as though looking for something—she didn't know what.

At last he swiveled her around so that her back was toward him. She heard him catch his breath and, in the mirror, she watched the taut expression on his face. He traced a leisurely path up her spine with his fingertip, leaving a thread of heat behind. She swayed. He pulled her back, slowly, until her curves fit perfectly against his hard body.

"Liz," he murmured again, the word like a caress. He buried his face at the side of her neck as his hands slid inside the dress to cup and mold her breasts. The heat from his hands spread to warm her whole body. Every nerve ending under the surface of her skin, every vein that carried blood to nourish her heart, throbbed with longing. Helplessly her head fell against his shoulder. When his fingers brushed her nipples she moaned aloud.

At the sound, Justin raised his eyes to meet hers in the mirror. He shook his head in an apparent attempt to remember where he was, to regain control over himself; she knew just how he felt. "Damn this party," he muttered. He withdrew his hands and fumbled slightly, and endearingly, with the zipper and the hooks. At last he had her fastened into her dress, and he turned her to face him.

Her palms rested lightly on his chest. She could feel his irregular heartbeat and heated skin through the fine white fabric of his shirt. "Can you tie a bow tie?" he asked.

It was the last thing she expected. Not only the question but the disquiet with which it was uttered. Justin disconcerted? Impossible.

Feeling an unexpected jolt of pleasure at the thought, she smiled. Her mind began to clear. Slowly the room returned to its normal state, no more uncanny, bizarre currents in the air. "Of course; my dad says that every woman should know how."

"Your father," he growled, his hands moving restlessly at her waist. "They'll be here any minute." He laughed, a low, sexy laugh. "He'd kill me if he caught me with my hands on you."

With a few deft twists she made a perfect bow. Keeping one hand at her waist, he turned halfway to look at her handiwork in the mirror. He touched the knot. "Thanks." Then he reached for the lei. "Aloha, Elizabeth," he said quietly, as he lifted it over her head.

When the cool, damp flowers came into contact with her heated skin, Liz was surprised not to hear a sizzle.

He kissed her ceremoniously on both cheeks. And then she was in his arms. His eyes blazed with some emotion she couldn't name, and one hand cradled her face, holding her motionless. His mouth came down to cover hers fiercely, wanting more.

Finally, he released her. He was breathing heavily. "You know we've reached a point where we have to make some decisions, don't you?"

"Yes, I know," she replied candidly. Her eyes were wide and dark. Her soft voice belied the storm that was raging inside her.

He touched her cheek and moved to the door.

She noticed that his knuckles were white on the knob. "I'll be down in a minute," she said.

He looked at her. She knew what he saw—a woman who was clearly reeling from the effects of his kiss.

His mouth quirked at one corner. "All right," he answered gently. Then he left.

Chapter Six

Liz entered the living room full of ambiguous feelings. Justin was standing beside the fireplace, a drink in his hand. Their eyes met for a brief second; she was the first to look away.

"Liz. Sweetheart." She turned gratefully toward her father's voice. He was resplendent in his dress uniform, and her mother looked smart and sensational in a dress of black silk.

"Daddy, Mother," Liz breathed as she moved forward without hesitation into her father's arms. He looked into her face and gave a satisfied nod before surrendering her to her mother's embrace. "You look pretty, honey," he pronounced.

Her mother, however, studied her with a keener eye,

and Liz waited for her to comment on the pallor she herself had noticed in the mirror.

Instead, Betsy said, "What a beautiful lei," and asked, "How is the work going?"

"Very well," Liz answered, relaxing. "I've gotten some really interesting material. I wish you'd stay over tonight."

Sondra, who was passing, heard the comment and stopped to add her urging to Liz's.

Liz imagined that she saw the two women exchange a knowledgeable look, then Betsy smiled at their hostess and the moment passed. "We appreciate the invitation, Sondra, but Robert has an important meeting in the morning."

"Bad timing," added Robert. "But we'll have to leave about ten."

"I'm flattered that you consented to come for the evening. You must come back soon," Sondra said warmly, before responding to a discreet gesture from Annie in the doorway. "Excuse me."

"Quick trip," observed Liz in a dry tone.

Her father harrumphed. "Well, you know how your mother worries about you, sweetheart. She had to make sure you were all right."

Betsy rolled her eyes and Liz digested a laugh. They both knew that it was the admiral who was the overprotective parent. Probably because he had always been gone from home so much, he felt bidden to take charge when he was there. They knew he cared about them and worried about them when he was away, but often the distance was so great, there was nothing he could do when an emergency arose. He had to rely on Betsy's strength and brains.

Images came to mind—her mother dabbing calamine lotion on itchy chicken pox, going from her room to James's all night long to keep them from scratching; driving like a demon to the emergency room with James bleeding all over the back seat after he was hit in the head by a flying Little League bat. Liz remembered the times her mother had handled the responsibility of moving the entire household, including cats, dogs and kids, because her husband was halfway around the world.

She and her mother had an unspoken agreement, allowing the admiral the illusion of being in charge. "Yes, Daddy, I know."

He nodded. "I think I'll sample the buffet," he said, and left them alone.

Betsy spoke. "Let's go out to the lanai. I want to talk to you."

Liz felt a moment's apprehension. It wasn't like her mother to be so serious-minded at a party. She'd been looking forward to seeing them. Now she wished they'd declined.

Her mother had always been a master at recognizing distress in her children, even when it wasn't severe distress, and even when they thought they'd hidden it well. She was more persistent than Justin and would never give up digging for the cause until she'd found it.

"Okay." Liz followed Betsy through the French doors. The lanai was deserted. Evidently, right now the food was more popular with Sondra's guests than the scenery.

Betsy found a chaise longue and made herself comfortable. Liz took a straight chair beside her.

"Now, tell me what's going on between you and Justin Hogan."

"Justin?" said Liz, a benign smile on her lips. "He's been very helpful."

"He's been more than that," said her mother flatly. "I saw the way he looked at you when you came into the room." Her mother settled deeper into the chaise. "And the way you looked at him," she added, her eyes keen on her daughter. "I could have fried eggs on air between you. I hadn't thought to ever see that expression in your eyes again, sweetheart. It makes me very happy."

It was a good thing Liz was sitting down. At her mother's words, her knees would have given way. How could she see... "Mother, please, you're misreading things." She forced an airy lack of concern into her remark, and was both pleased and surprised when it came out sounding that way. She went on, "Justin Hogan is an attractive man. Maybe if the circumstances were different... but he and I have nothing in common."

"What does that have to do with anything?" asked her mother, clearly confounded.

"He and I live such different lives. I love my work, but it requires me to travel so much. He stays in one spot. Even if he wanted to, he couldn't take off; the responsibilities here are too great. I wouldn't be happy doing anything else." She laughed lightly. "You, of all people, should understand that, Mother. We're all alike, you, Daddy, me, James. We're all nomads."

Her mother was taken aback. "I'm not," she said. "Certainly not by choice."

Liz stared.

"I'm a nomad only because your father chose the navy as his career. Did you really think I *enjoy* being apart from him for months, years at a time? I would like nothing better than to stay in one place for the rest of my life, to plant a garden and see it flourish, to have close friends today that will still be close ten years from now."

"But you've always seemed to thrive on the life," Liz said weakly. "You've jumped right into everything new each time we moved and made it all an adventure. If there wasn't a club for the wives on the base, you organized one; if the housing was bland, you spiced it up. And you did it all so cheerfully."

"Of course I did—I do. But that's what life handed me when I fell in love with your father. It isn't travel, it certainly isn't the moving, it isn't the life that I love, honey—it's the man." She leaned forward and covered her daughter's hand with her own. "Liz, darling, your father has always been very important in your life, but don't make the mistake of thinking you have to fall in love with someone just like him.''

Liz took a moment to consider. She wasn't sure she agreed with her mother. One grew accustomed to a way of life and it wasn't easy to change. Even if she did fall in love with Justin—which she wouldn't, she reminded herself. Or he with her—even more of a long shot. "It doesn't matter, anyway. There's still my job.''

"Of course,'' Betsy readily concurred. "And only you can decide whether you can adapt the life-style that your job requires to another person's.''

Liz touched her temple. She hoped she wasn't getting a headache. "Mother, I keep telling you it isn't relevant.''

"Maybe not. I hope I've given you something to think about, however.''

Liz was quiet for a minute. "You have,'' she finally admitted.

"Then it was worth the trip. Now, we'd probably better rejoin the others,'' said her mother.

The rest of the evening passed pleasantly. Liz put her mother's words out of her mind for now. It was something she would have to meditate over when she was alone, when there were no distractions.

She was even civil to Babs, who was civil back. The meeting, which she had dreaded, was brief and forgettable.

Poor Jay was more disturbed by the blonde than Liz was. She felt sorry for him as she watched him hover.

Babs Tremaine wasn't the sort of woman a nice fellow like Jay should fall in love with.

The next morning Liz woke feeling confused. For a moment she couldn't remember why, then her eyes landed on the lei. Memories of the previous evening rushed in, overflowing her mind—the scene with Justin in her bedroom, the conversation with her mother.

She pushed the thoughts away and climbed out of bed. Last night she had been asleep as soon as her head hit the pillow but today she had to do some thinking.

Was her mother right? Could the assumptions she'd always felt guided by be wrong? She had assumed the man for her, whenever he came, would be a military man like her father, that they would live an exciting, if unsettled, life, that they would travel and she would take her pictures, that they would live and bring up their family in the far-flung places of the earth. It was what she knew, after all, what she was accustomed to.

Now she wondered. Had she been too immersed in that picture to look at Taylor with objective eyes? It was a sad thought. Maybe he had fit the image she'd constructed, and that was all. Maybe she never loved him as her mother loved her father. She certainly had never responded to his kisses as she had to Justin's, with desire and abandon. That reaction was not to be ignored.

Common sense told her that mere desire was as dangerous a reason for marriage as deciding to marry someone because he fit a pattern. One thing was certain, she wouldn't find the objectivity she was seeking if Justin was nearby. He had a more potent effect on her than she'd ever thought any man could, especially after the debacle with Taylor. What she needed was room to think; what she needed was distance.

While she dressed in jeans and a cool white shirt, she weighed the pros and cons of remaining at the house or moving to a hotel. It was the busiest time of the tourist season, but surely she could find someplace to stay.

Absently she picked up her nightshirt from the bed and started to fold it, but her hands stilled as she stared through the open doors. She didn't see the ancient banyan tree, didn't see the rolling landscape. Instead she saw Justin's face, and Sondra's.

Sondra would demand explanations if Liz moved to a hotel; she would be troubled, maybe offended. On the other hand, Liz would be free of the growing tension between her and Justin.

Liz sank onto the mattress, her nightshirt twisted around her clenched fists, and her eyes went again, unbidden, to the lei. The memory of last night, before the party—the sensuality that radiated from him like body heat—made her pulse leap with anticipation.

Finally she made up her mind. She dropped the nightshirt onto the bed and grabbed her brush from the dresser. She brushed her flaming hair until her eyes stung, pulled the mass into a tortoiseshell clasp at her nape and left the room.

From the upstairs hall the house sounded strangely quiet, and by the time she reached the bottom of the steps she knew that something was definitely amiss. Though the house was never noisy, there was always a sound here and there, a feeling of hidden activity. This morning there was nothing.

She walked through the empty rooms to the kitchen. No one was there. At the back entrance she peered through the glass panes. Justin stood near a pickup truck parked in the drive talking to two men. Sondra and Annie were with him. As she watched one of the men took a bag from the truck and walked with Justin in the direction of the stables. Annie and the other man went off in another direction, and Sondra came slowly toward the house.

A coffee mug dangled from her fingers. Liz could see, even at this distance, the worried frown on her face. Her footsteps seemed to drag, and when she reached the back entrance Liz automatically opened the door for her.

Sondra gave a distracted smile. "Thank you, my dear."

"Is there something wrong, Sondra?" Liz asked.

Sondra sighed. "Yes, but we're not sure how serious it is. There are some cows down in the south pasture. The vet from Hilo just arrived and Justin is taking him out to have a look at them."

Liz knew nothing about cattle operations, but if the expressions on the faces of the five people gathered around the truck were anything to go on, they were very worried. "Who was the man with Annie?"

"That's her husband, John. He's Justin's foreman."

"Annie's married?" Liz didn't know why she was surprised.

Sondra nodded. "Very much so. John is the ranch foreman and Justin's right hand. When my husband died so unexpectedly, John held this place together while Justin learned everything he needed to know to take over." She went to the coffee maker and refilled her cup. Then she held up the pot; the tired gesture was accompanied by an inquiring lift of her brow. "Have you had coffee? Annie won't be in for a while, I'm afraid. She went home to feed John. He and Justin have been up all night. If you're hungry—I'm not a great cook, but I can scramble eggs."

Liz took the pot from her and reached for a mug. "Nonsense, Sondra. I'm not used to being waited on. As a matter of fact, I'm a pretty good cook myself. Why don't I fix breakfast?"

Sondra took her cup to the table and sat staring out through the bay window. "That would be nice, dear," she murmured as though she'd forgotten Liz was there. Her face was drawn with something more than worry, something that to Liz looked very much like grief. For the first time since Liz had met her Sondra looked her age. What could she say, what could she do to ease her worries?

Activity was the only answer she could come up with. She went to the refrigerator and removed the makings for a meal. In a few minutes, she had bacon frying in an iron skillet, eggs whipped to a light frothiness, and toast buttered and ready for the broiler. She hesitated, then decided to wait before finishing.

Sondra roused herself when Liz refilled both coffee cups and joined her at the table. "Thank you, dear. I'm sorry, I—" Her voice broke.

Liz had no intention of prying, but when Sondra spoke again, she listened with interest, curious to find out what had laid this vital woman low. "My husband was killed in an accident during just such an emergency as this."

Liz hid her shock. She felt a flood of sympathy but didn't know how to express it; it was as though she'd entered unexpectedly into a home shadowed by sorrow. All she could do was to be here, to listen.

"It was years ago, of course," Sondra went on. "With modern methods, surely this won't turn into a full-blown crisis. Back then it took weeks to determine the cause. They had to dispose of the diseased cattle quickly and keep a close watch on the others...." She choked on a sob and turned to Liz with a look of distress, tears wetting her cheeks.

"Oh, Sondra," Liz whispered, fighting her own tears. Instinctively she reached out to cover Sondra's hand. It was ice cold.

Sondra was immediately contrite. "I'm sorry, my dear. I didn't mean to put my burdens on you. It's just that this brings it all back ... and makes me terrified for my son."

"Please don't apologize, Sondra," said Liz gently. "Would it be easier on you if I went to a hotel?"

"It would certainly be easier on you, Liz. Things will be rather hectic around here until this is over. But I'd like for you to stay."

"Then I'll stay," Liz agreed immediately. So circumstances were to dictate her choice after all.

She rose and went to the stove to turn the bacon. She had reduced the flame beneath the pan when the sound of a truck's engine from the direction of the barn reached her ears.

"There's the truck. They're back. Justin will be hungry," said Sondra.

Liz slid the toast into the oven and gave the eggs a last swipe with the wooden spoon before pouring them into a pan she had readied. Sondra set the table. When Justin came in a few minutes later they turned as though in tandem.

He eyed Liz's apron with a frown, but without comment, before he closed the door behind him.

Liz was suddenly self-conscious. She dropped her gaze to the eggs she was stirring.

Sondra had hurried to her son's side. "How bad is it, Justin?"

Justin took off his Stetson and hooked it on a coat tree by the back door. "We don't know yet. The vet has taken some blood samples back to his lab. He'll call me with the results as soon as possible." He ran a tired hand over his face. "Is that bacon I smell?"

"Yes, dear. Liz cooked breakfast, but we waited for you."

"I'll clean up and be right with you," he said. But instead, he came over to where Liz was standing. He planted his hands on his hips, pulling his stained blue work shirt taut across his broad chest. She looked into his eyes, trying to read the expression there.

"You can cook?" he asked.

She didn't react to his skeptical tone. "Yes," she answered and calmly went back to her task.

Justin watched her for another moment; she could feel the weight of his gaze, the impact of his nearness. Finally, silently, he turned and left the room. Liz exhaled. Why was he so guarded this morning? When he returned a few minutes later she was putting the toast into a napkin-lined basket.

"I had to cancel our trip to the mountain today," he said as he slid into his chair.

"Of course," said Liz, setting the basket before him. She was surprised that he would even mention it. She had forgotten about the trip.

"I'm sorry about this. Maybe you'd like to move to a hotel."

Liz's jaw dropped.

Sondra gasped, "Justin! Don't be rude. Liz has already agreed to stay—at my request," she finished pointedly.

He mumbled something that Liz didn't ask him to repeat and reached for the toast.

Annie was back in her kitchen well before lunchtime. Liz volunteered to help and Annie sent her out to do the marketing, armed with two lists, one for the house and a much longer one for the bunkhouse. Justin had hired extra hands to help out during the emergency.

When she returned an hour later, the back seat of her rental car was crammed with sacks of groceries. She laughed as she elbowed her way into the kitchen carrying a sack in each arm. "I hope Justin's hired an army," she said. "We have enough to feed one."

"Just about," agreed Annie. "I'll call Curly, the cook, to come pick up his part."

"Why unload it all twice? We can take out what you need and I'll deliver the rest."

"Justin wouldn't like that; you're a guest," Annie told her tightly.

It was obvious he'd said something to Annie. Liz had to grit her teeth to keep from responding inappropriately. "Not much of a guest if I can't pitch in when there's a problem. Have you heard anything more about the cattle?"

"No, not a thing." Annie still looked dubious.

"Honestly, Annie," Liz said, putting her hands on her hips in exasperation. "If it will make you feel better, Justin will never know that I delivered groceries to the bunkhouse."

"Okay. I'll give Curly a call and tell him to expect you."

Liz maneuvered the car out of the driveway and reversed, heading toward the huge barn. A road, really more of a track, circled the building and climbed a gentle rise to a dormitory-style building.

A short, plump man came out the door. "Mornin', ma'am. You must be Miz Ennis."

Liz gave him a friendly smile and climbed out of the car. "And you must be Curly," she said, eyeing his bald head with amusement. They unloaded the groceries and Curly showed her around his kitchen. She marveled at the convenience of the space. Huge pots simmered on the stove and a vast counter covered with jumbo appliances attested to the size of the crowd he fed. "How many do you cook for?" she asked him.

"Ordinarily, about sixty or so. But when Mr. Hogan hires on extra men, like today, I'll probably feed a hundred," he told her, laughing at her amazement. He walked her to her car, thanking her profusely.

She was steering the car around the corner of the barn when she looked up to see Justin standing squarely in her path. His fists were planted on his hips; a glower—worse than a frown—darkened the handsome face. Her foot jammed at the brake and the car came to a stop inches from those long legs. Her heart threatened to jump from her chest. She let her head drop forward to rest on her hands, which still clenched the steering wheel as though cemented there. She took a long, deep breath.

"Where have you been?" demanded Justin from the open window beside her.

Instead of answering, she whipped her head around and glared. "You numbskull, I almost hit you! Are you crazy?"

He wrenched the door open. "Sometimes I think so. Move over."

Liz was more than glad to remove her rigid fingers from the steering wheel. She moved the gearshift into park and slid across the seat.

Justin got in, slammed the door and put the car in gear. "I asked you a question."

She flexed her stiff fingers and shrugged with more dismissiveness than she felt. She sent a silent apology to Annie. "I was delivering groceries to Curly."

"Damn it, you're a guest—not a delivery boy."

"And obviously you've given orders to that effect—which is the most childish thing I've ever heard," she snapped. "You and your mother have fed and housed me. The least I can do is help out now."

He didn't answer. The firm, disciplined jaw was clenched in frustration. Liz looked closely at him for the first time since he'd gotten into the car. His clothes were grimy with dirt and perspiration. The lines around his eyes were deep with worry and fatigue. Annie had told her that the afflicted cows were discovered around midnight, so he hadn't slept at all last night. Her eyes were drawn to his big hands. The knuckles of one were scraped and blood had dried across them. She felt her heart squeeze.

The short ride was soon over. Justin pulled her car into the garage beside a blue Lincoln sedan and switched off the motor. It was cooler, quieter here, out of the sun.

His voice was deceptively calm when he spoke again. "This is what ranch life is like—completely self-focused. The ranch, the cattle have to come first. Social plans are often canceled and on occasion things get very dirty and gritty, even dangerous. I suppose Mother told you about my dad's death."

"Part of it," she answered quietly. "She worries about you, too."

He stared through the windshield. "I was afraid this would bring it all back to haunt her. I was away at school when it happened. A few cows got sick, then a few more. Dad was so worried that we might lose the whole herd. He was a great horseman, but he was close to sixty and out of shape. After a week of sleepless nights, his reflexes were slow. His horse stumbled and rolled on top of him." Justin made a sound that may have been a sigh. "His neck was broken—he died instantly."

Liz caught her breath. *This has brought it all back to you as well as your mother,* she observed, *but, strong man that you are, you mustn't let that show.* Suddenly she understood. Instead of giving in to his sorrow over his father's death and sharing his apprehension about the ranch, he'd focused on something totally irrelevant, like inconvenience to a guest.

"Mother is a strong woman in most ways, but some things are difficult for her to deal with, and trouble on the ranch is one of them. I think she would really like to leave the ranch—to move to California and live near my sister." He took off his hat and thrust his fingers through his hair before replacing the hat firmly, pulling the brim down to shadow his eyes. "Liz, I know your job comes first, but . . ."

Liz opened her mouth in protest but he turned to pin her with a look and went on, "Having another woman around..." He took a deep breath and looked away. "Since my mother asked you to stay, I would appreciate it if you would."

She remained very still under his gaze, but she recognized what the request had cost him. For a reason she didn't understand, he was reluctant—no, he was *resentful*—about asking her for help. Still she didn't hesitate to offer it. "I'll stay until things get back to normal." Her heart was full. If he could just loosen this tight hold he kept on himself—

"Normal? I doubt that things will ever be back to normal around here," he barked.

They both got out of the car and she faced him across the roof. "Then I'll stay until you tell me to go," she said.

Something flashed hot in those green eyes. She chose not to let it register, and finally he simply nodded.

She walked out of the garage. Justin was a hard man, but a strong one.

When she'd first arrived at Fairwinds, Liz had fallen in love with the house but, unfamiliar as she was with the workings of a big operation like this one, had never been quite comfortable when she explored other parts of the property. Not for the first time she realized that, despite the beauty of the place, it was run like big business.

Over the next few days she learned her way around. Though most of her time was spent with Sondra, she pitched in wherever she was needed. She drove the pickup truck out to the pasture where the men worked; she delivered lunch, or cold beer, or messages. She helped Annie in the kitchen and house, though housework was kept to a minimum to free hands for more important tasks. And she found that she liked being a part of it all, liked being able to help.

Friday afternoon, she approached Justin as he was leaving the house after a quick meal. They had barely said ten words to each other in the past five days. She followed him outside, reluctant to intrude on his concern. But the drama, as it unfolded, of a ranch in peril would be extraordinary material for a photographic essay already forming in her head.

"Justin," she called.

He paused, waiting while she caught up with him, and shortened his steps to accommodate hers as they continued toward the barn. "How are you holding up?" he asked. He was trying to be genial, but the exhaustion seeped into his smile. His voice sounded hoarse.

"I'm fine." She didn't ask how he was; he would only lie. She hesitated. "I have a favor to ask, Justin. Call it my second wish if you like," she told him.

"What is it?" he asked.

"I wonder if you'd let me photograph the men as they work."

Justin looked at Liz, clean and beautiful, and thought about the filthy, exhausted men out in the pastures. He felt pretty much like a grub, himself, now that he thought about it. He ran a hand over his stubbled chin. "When are you supposed to leave for India?" he asked, instead of responding to her request.

The question caught her by surprise; she hadn't even thought of India, or of leaving. "Not until the first of the month. Why?"

Justin shrugged. He hoped he was the only one who knew the effort it caused him to be casual. She had a penetrating way of looking at a man. "Just curious. Sure—you can take pictures."

He'd noticed with a certain rueful guilt that she'd tried to stay out of his way since the crisis had started—she probably thought he would repeat his childish admonition that she was a guest here—but he'd noticed also how much help she'd been to Annie and how much a comfort to his mother.

They had reached the shadow of the barn, but she made no move to return to the house. He could use some of her comfort himself, he realized.

The wind picked up. One current caught a strand of her hair and tossed it carelessly over her shoulder. In the wake of another breeze, one of the barn doors swung silently on its hinges.

"Aren't you going to warn me not to get in the way?" she asked, stuffing her hands into the back pockets of her jeans.

A single light shone from inside the building, highlighting the honest radiance of her profile. She was so damned beautiful. But there was a lot more to this woman than beauty; she had courage. No one who went into the places her job took her to lacked courage.

As he looked at her, he had an almost unstoppable urge to wrap his arms around her, to bury his face in the soft, sweet curve of her neck and sleep the sleep of the weary. He laughed silently to himself. If he could look at that beautiful body—long legs and sweet butt in those tight jeans, high breasts defined under the thin cotton blouse—and think of sleep, something must be very wrong with him. He raised one of his gloved hands to catch the door, which had started to close again.

Liz saw the amusement soften his features and, while she wondered at the reason, she was glad that some of the awful fatigue had drained away.

He lifted a dark brow. "Is that what brother James would say?"

"'Fraid so," she admitted with a tentative smile.

"Well, that's where we differ. I think a professional photographer, who's been where you've been and done the things you've done, would know enough to stay out of the way without being warned."

Her smile grew soft at his show of confidence.

Justin couldn't resist. He leaned forward and covered her smile with an easy, gentle kiss.

Liz's eyes drifted shut. It was the sweetest kiss they'd ever shared. She slid her hands out of her pockets and placed them on his chest, but before she could move closer, his fingers gripped the barn door tightly and he straightened. For an instant she wondered if she was being rejected, but then he smiled, too.

"I don't want to start something I can't finish," he said huskily.

She nodded, stepped back and returned her hands to her pockets. "May I borrow a horse?"

At that, he did frown, and she went on before he could speak. "I won't be a burden, I promise."

"Liz, I can't spare a man ..."

"No one has to wait on me, Justin."

He exhaled. "What was it your daddy said? That you could talk anyone into anything?"

"No, he said I can talk to anyone about anything."

"I like my version better."

She persisted. "I know how to groom and care for a horse. I can saddle my own mount and rub him down afterward."

He thought for a minute. "I don't let anyone ride my horses without checking out their horsemanship first."

Liz bristled at that, but before she could protest he grinned, touched the end of her nose with a finger and added, "Be here at six tomorrow morning."

Chapter Seven

Liz's mount was a beautiful chestnut mare with a white star between her eyes. While Justin adjusted the length of the stirrups, Liz leaned forward, stroking the horse's neck. "I'll bet her name is Star."

In the early morning light, he grinned at her and dipped under the mare's neck to work on the opposite side. "Give us some credit for imagination. My sister named her Beth."

"Beth doesn't seem to be a particularly imaginative name to me," she teased. "But now I know why you picked her for me."

He finished and gave the horse an affectionate pat. "Ah, but this baby's name isn't short for Elizabeth."

"No?"

"No. Her name is Bethlehem."

Liz laughed. "Whatever her name is, she's a beauty."

Justin transferred his hand from the horse's rump to Liz's knee. "You haven't ridden in a while, have you?"

She shook her head. "No, but—"

He diverted the protest. "I'm not going to renege. I was just going to say, we'll take it easy. Let me know if you get tired."

Liz tried to ignore the heat from his hand. "I didn't ask for permission to shoot so that I could slow you down, Justin," she said truthfully. "I'll bargain with you. I won't get in your way, and you won't worry about me."

He patted her knee absently and mounted his big black Arabian with an agility that was surprising in a man so large. He took the lead, but after a few miles he signaled with a thumbs-up that she was on her own. He turned the black and headed to the barn where, she knew, he had an appointment with a representative of the state agricultural inspector.

Liz made her way to the south pasture, where the first cows had fallen. When she'd found a spot good for observing but out of the way, she reached into the saddlebags for her camera. She worked through lunch.

The virus had been pinpointed in a laboratory and a vaccine imported from the mainland. But the mass graves, the inoculation of thousands of head of cattle, the blood, sweat and tears of the cowboys provided a stark contrast to the legendary beauty of the island. All this provided the background for her record of the episode.

The images of the men were strong and vigorous. The images of the animals were melancholy and tragic but, recorded by her camera, they would all make a powerful statement.

Finally, on Saturday, the vet pronounced the situation under control at last. By then forty-seven cows had been buried. Saturday was also the day Babs came.

During breakfast, Justin returned to the house wearing the tired smile of a victor. He entered the kitchen door, sailed his hat toward its accustomed hook and said, "It isn't over yet, but the vet thinks we've licked the worst of it. The incubation period of the virus is twenty-four hours. We haven't lost a head in forty-eight hours."

"Justin, I'm so relieved," said Sondra.

"Yeah, me, too." He gave his mother a hug and smiled at Liz. "We'll have our trip up the mountain, too, maybe tomorrow." He rubbed the stubble across his jaw. "Right now, I need to get cleaned up."

Sondra patted his tanned cheek. "And have a proper rest."

Justin delayed answering just long enough for the drawn, worried look to return to his mother's face. "The men are rechecking the herds to make sure the inoculations are holding up. I'll lie down for a while on the sofa in the study but I have to go out again, Mother.''

"Now, Justin...?''

Liz watched the scene between mother and son with an empty feeling of longing and loss. The emergency was over; her work—at least her essay on the crisis— was finished. She couldn't be sure, because she hadn't been into town to the lab yet and the film rested undeveloped in her bag, but the essay might be the best thing she'd ever done.

The only remaining shots for the Visitors' Bureau job were to be taken of the Kona Coast, on the opposite side of the island. Kailua-Kona was too far to commute to from Fairwinds; she would have to move into a hotel.

And Justin would leave soon for Texas. She knew the trip was important.

There were so many possibilities for a relationship between them, and so many barriers. If only she weren't a dyed-in-the-wool itinerant. If only he weren't tied to his land with absolute and unbreakable bonds. She felt guilty for thinking such a thing after just having witnessed his untiring efforts to save the unfortunate animals, his responsibility toward the men.

Soon she would have to leave, pick up her life again. The prospect left her deeply disturbed.

Neither Sondra nor Justin had noticed her discomfort. Sondra had argued, but given in. "I suppose I'll have to be satisfied with your sleeping on the sofa then," she was saying. "If I weren't here you wouldn't do that much, would you?"

Justin gave Sondra a hug. "Nope. But you're such a domineering mother...."

"Oh, you." Sondra slapped at him playfully. "Go shower. You smell to high heaven."

"Yes, ma'am," he said with mock obeisance. He winked at Liz and disappeared.

A few hours later, Liz stood in the broad entrance hall, wondering what to do with Babs Tremaine. Sondra had gone to her room, Annie was in the kitchen, so she had answered the front doorbell.

Babs had sauntered in looking gorgeous in a pair of pale green slacks and a clingy green and navy knit top, which Liz thought was a bit obvious. But that might just be spite, she acknowledged. The blonde's make-up was flawless, reminding Liz that she hadn't bothered with any.

"Is Justin here?" Babs had asked coolly, ignoring a greeting of any kind. "I need to see him. It's important."

Liz bit her lip, wondering if she should send Babs to his study. Finally she said, "Have a seat. I'll see."

"Thank you." Babs went into the living room to wait.

Liz headed for the study with a wry smile on her face. She knocked softly but there was no answer so she opened the door.

Justin was on the sofa, his head resting on the back cushion and his long legs crossed at the ankles and propped on the coffee table in front of him. It didn't look like the most comfortable position, but he was sleeping the sleep of exhaustion. He had showered and shaved and was dressed in clean work clothes.

Quietly Liz closed the door and stood looking at him, longing to smooth the lines from his face. Suddenly her feelings were in chaos. The thought of leaving this man was unbearable. But she had to leave; she had a commitment. The call she had told Justin about the night she arrived had come on Monday. The editorial board of *Geography Today* had okayed the follow-up on India.

At last, still fighting her uncontrolled feelings, she knelt beside the sofa and touched his cheek. "Justin," she said quietly.

His hand came up to capture hers against his face but he slept on.

"Justin, wake up. Babs is here, she says it's important that she see you."

He opened his eyes. For a moment, the expression there was unguarded as they stared at each other. It was unlike the heated looks he usually gave her. There was something else in his gaze, something much more profound—like . . . maybe . . . love?

Liz's pulse gave a jolt and began to race. But before she could start to analyze her reaction, the telephone rang and his expression closed to her. He swung his legs off the table and crossed to his desk. "Hello."

He listened for a moment, then he turned to her, holding out the receiver. "It's for you. Your editor."

She approached to take the receiver from him. As their fingers brushed, he gave her a self-mocking, cheerless smile. The smile was brief; she might have misread it, but she put her hand over the mouthpiece. "Justin," she whispered, her voice soft and quivering.

"I'll see what Babs wants while you take your call," he said.

After finishing her call—concerning travel vouchers, of all things—Liz remained in the study for a minute, trying to reclaim the warmth in Justin's eyes when he'd wakened. She'd never seen that look before. It was an unspoken admission that his emotions were both deeper and more profound than just a sexual itch. And she had felt her heart open to him like a flower to the sun.

During the emergency with the cattle, Sondra's dinner party faded into history, but not her mother's surprising revelations. Now, they replayed in her thoughts as clearly as though they'd been recorded on videotape. "It isn't the life, it's the man," Betsy had said. So much had happened since that night.

She laughed to herself. So much had happened since she arrived at Fairwinds. At first she had enjoyed the ranch as she enjoyed all new experiences; she had admired the house, its beauty and its ambience; but she hadn't felt as attached, as much a part of the place as she did now. Somehow, during the crisis, when she'd pitched in to help, she had gathered a bit of the place to her, as her own.

It isn't the life, it's the man. She shook her head to clear her thoughts and left the study. She didn't want to be alone. Annie was in the kitchen, tearing lettuce into a bowl for salad.

"Can I help?" asked Liz.

Annie smiled at her. "Lunch is just about ready, but you could set the table in the dining room." She told Liz where to find linens and silverware.

Over the past few days, they had eaten all their meals in the kitchen and mostly on the run. Liz interpreted the return to formality as another signal that the routine would soon be back to normal.

"Thank you, Liz," Annie said as she left the room.

Liz smiled poignantly. Annie hadn't bothered with thanks during the crisis, either.

Liz moved around the table, arranging the cutwork place mats on the gleaming surface of the table. Idly she glanced out the window.

And froze.

When Justin returned to the house after seeing Babs on her way, he glanced through to the dining room to see Liz setting the table, her back to him. Her blazing hair tumbled down her back, set afire by the sunlight streaming through the window; his pulse began to pound like a jackhammer. The news he had just received should appease her silly suspicion of Babs, whatever it was.

Tonight he'd turn in early, catch up on the sleep he'd missed. Tomorrow they would ride up the mountain—he regretted that Babs and Jay were going along, but they'd already been invited—and the next day he had to leave. He could not fly out of here without some important questions answered.

What he was about to do might be a risk but it was one he had to take, and he had to take it today. He couldn't wait. The trip to Texas had already been postponed once. He couldn't put it off any longer and she could be half a world away before he got home. God only knew when he'd find her again.

Justin was no stranger to taking risks. Asking Liz here had been a big risk; ranching itself was a risky business. This one, however, was the biggest—he could scare her off.

Liz wasn't going to take kindly to any suggestion that would limit her freedom. Still, after the moment in his study, the extraordinary moment when he'd opened his eyes and looked into the face of love, he was hopeful. Hopeful? Hell. He was confident.

Smiling like a foolish kid, he entered the dining room. He felt a bit slaphappy; it was the weariness, he supposed. Or it was the contemplation of finally having Elizabeth Ennis securely in his life? He vowed to himself that he wouldn't press her but if she'd just give him an ounce of encouragement ... "Liz—"

Her shoulders tensed reflexively at the sound of his voice. She ignored him, didn't turn, didn't speak. He hesitated, frowning, wondering what the hell could have happened in the past ten minutes. He hadn't misread her response in the study. Surely not. The phone call? No, he understood her commitment to her work. He searched his mind for a reason, but none came.

Suddenly, his eyes went to the window, returned to Liz and went to the window again. A hollow cavity opened up inside him.

Damn it. This was ridiculous. "I told you once before, Babs is *not* my girlfriend," he snapped.

Liz glanced over her shoulder, her skepticism clear.

He crossed the room in two strides. He grabbed her by the upper arms and forced her to look at him.

He stared. The beautiful blue-green eyes that a short time ago had shone with love were now dry and disillusioned.

"No, damn it! You can't believe that," he almost shouted. Then he lowered his voice to a reasonable level. "Liz, listen to me." His hands moved restlessly on her arms, but she was not responding.

Suddenly, he knew he was fighting for his very life. "Liz, darling, I love you. I want to marry you." He pulled her into his arms. His fingers tangled in her hair as his big hand held her head possessively to his chest. He kissed her forehead, her eyes, her cheeks; her skin was soft under his lips. "You feel so good next to me, Liz. You belong there, you know you do. I love you."

His husky voice sent rivers of longing through Liz. She fought bravely against the feelings his declaration of love produced. She would have given her life to have heard those words ten minutes ago, she realized.

But when he tilted her head to seek her lips she turned aside with a frantic movement. If that mouth found hers, she would be lost. "Justin, wait." She pushed against his chest.

For a second, she didn't think he would release her. He seemed to be fighting some battle within himself, but then he dropped his arms.

Justin watched her retreat from him with a feeling akin to abandonment. Her expression did not yield one iota. Her face was blank.

"I'm not the kind of wife you need," she said evenly.

"You don't have to give up your career," he said, almost desperately. "We can work something out, Liz. And you don't have to give me an answer right now. Just tell me you'll think about it. Please."

The "please" almost got her. Liz knew how he hated to ask for anything.

When she had looked out the window and seen Babs in Justin's arms she had almost cried aloud at the pain that shattered her so suddenly and unexpectedly. She felt as though she were completely unarmed and under attack. Attack? The feeling was more like a bombardment. Her eyes had burned; her throat had closed. When she finally was able to draw a breath, she was surprised to find her heart still beating. But she couldn't look away.

The scene in the study...the expansive gap in her control over her emotions...she had sworn to herself that she would never relinquish her heart, and there she was, trusting a man again, she thought bitterly. She was even on the verge of setting aside her career in favor of another. But now she knew the truth—had known the truth from the moment she'd looked outside.

The scene was imprinted on her brain. Babs had been smiling and talking, gesturing toward the house occasionally. As she watched, Justin had grinned and opened his arms.

The diminutive blonde promptly flung herself into them. He lifted her feet off the ground, whirled her around. When he set her down, he looked at her for a minute; then he kissed her tenderly. That was the climax—his obvious tenderness toward the woman in his arms, the woman who had hurt Liz so deeply. He couldn't know that she had once seen Babs Tremaine in another man's arms, but she had, and she couldn't erase the image from her mind, though it had been dimmed by this one.

Justin might care for her, he might want to marry her, but at the sight of that tender kiss she recognized clearly that she was his second choice. And, God help her, if she was to be alone for the rest of her life, if she was to become a dried-up old prune of a woman, unloved and unwed, she would *never* be second to that woman again. And she would never let the woman be the catalyst for her tears.

"Justin, I'm very flattered. But it's not possible," she said tonelessly. Then she turned away. She reached out to grip the back of a chair.

Justin looked at her. Her shoulders, her spine were inflexible. "If you're refusing me because of what you thought you saw, because of Babs, she's decided to reconcile with her husband," he said after a minute. God, he was begging. He couldn't believe he was begging.

Liz didn't think her heart would endure another impact, but it did and it continued to beat regularly. As soon as Babs had told him, he'd decided to ask Liz to marry him. The timing was priceless. Second choice. She remained rigid. "I won't marry you."

"He's coming down from Oahu the day after tomorrow to take her back with him."

She was grateful that she wasn't facing him. The longer this went on, the more evidence of exhaustion crept into his voice; and the scene became infinitely bittersweet. Why didn't he just leave?

Annie bustled into the room carrying a large salad bowl. "Justin, I'm glad you're here. For once I won't have to track you down. Lunch is ready."

There was a long, deathly silence in the room. Annie hesitated and looked from one of them to the other.

Justin drew himself up to his full height. He looked once more at Liz's back and muttered, "I'm not hungry." He turned and strode from the room.

"I'll call Sondra," said Liz faintly when the sound of his footsteps had faded.

Liz was up at dawn. She called the hotel across the island at Kailua-Kona and made a reservation for the next night. While she read off her credit card number and waited for the computer to allocate a confirmation number, she gave herself a mental lecture.

With any luck at all she could be through with this assignment in a day or two and on the plane to New Delhi inside a week. Halfway around the world from Justin Hogan, and maybe, just maybe, her shattered heart could begin to heal. It had healed before, hadn't it? She'd lived through one emotional storm; she could live through another.

She replaced the telephone in its cradle and let her shoulders sag. Who was she kidding? Getting over Taylor had been a cinch compared to what it would be to get over Justin. If she ever did.

An hour later, dressed in jeans and a yellow gingham shirt, Liz went downstairs to fix herself a cup of coffee. When it was ready she took it onto the terrace, where she sat on a low wall and stared at her feet. Her heart was like a broken stone in her chest. This was the last day she would spend with Justin.

This would be the last night she would spend under his roof. Tomorrow he would leave for the mainland and she would leave for the Kona Coast. By the time he returned, she would be gone from the islands. Forever, she fervently hoped.

When she looked at the upcoming trip from one perspective, she was convinced that she couldn't bear to be near him for so many unbroken hours today. He had said they wouldn't be back until about four. From another angle, she found, to her bewilderment, she wanted to cherish each second.

"Good morning."

The deep voice set off a series of tremors along her nerve ends. She looked over her shoulder. He was watching her over the rim of a coffee mug. "Good morning." She was surprised at how natural she sounded. "Did you sleep well?"

Justin's free hand went up to massage the nape of his neck. "Pretty well," he said. Actually sleep had been impossible. As tired as he was, whenever he closed his eyes he had been haunted by images of her.

"Justin, we don't have to go riding today."

The hell we don't, thought Justin. Tomorrow he would leave for Dallas, and when he returned she would be gone. He dreaded the empty place she would leave in his home, in his heart.

Today was his last shot and he was damned well going to take advantage of every minute. They hadn't talked this through. Somehow he was going to convince her—somehow, sometime, today or tonight— that what they had going for them was rare.

He had to make her see that if they threw these feelings away, neither of them would ever have a chance like this again. Somehow he had to convince her of that. He opened his mouth to reply, but unexpectedly his mother did it for him.

"Nonsense," said Sondra, who had come out of the door behind them. "The others are already here. I saw Jay's car pull around to the barn. This is your last opportunity to photograph the glen, Liz, and it will do Justin good to get off the place for a few hours. He needs a break, don't you, dear?"

Her enthusiasm was a bit excessive this morning, thought Justin, as she shot his mother a suspicious look. She smiled sweetly. They were the same arguments she'd used last night when Liz had first tried to get out of the trip with a mention of some film she needed to develop.

Neither Liz nor Justin had had the heart to prick Sondra's good mood. Though they hadn't discussed her anxieties since the morning the crisis began, they both realized that the past few days had taken their toll on Sondra. She had aged noticeably.

Last night at dinner, though, they could both see that she was beginning to pull out of the depression that had almost paralyzed her during the emergency. Their eyes had met across the dinner table when she insisted they proceed with their plans. There had been an unspoken agreement, signed by the exchange of wary glances, to set aside their personal feelings rather than hint to Sondra of the hostility between them.

Justin sighed and set his mug on a table. "You're right, Mother. I'm on my way to saddle the horses," he told Liz. "I'll meet you there."

Liz joined the others at the barn. The first thing she noticed was that Jay wore a downtrodden expression. Poor Jay.

Babs's eyes were red-rimmed, as though she had been crying. Liz wondered, but she didn't much care, why.

Justin looked as grim as Liz felt. This should be some kind of day, she thought wryly, looking around at them.

At least the horses were eager, and they let them stretch their legs as they cantered over the pastures that surrounded Fairwinds. As the sun rose in the sky, however, Justin slowed the pace. Often they had to walk the animals along narrow trails. The morning wore on and the party climbed steadily, until suddenly they broke from a dense forest into blazing sunshine. They paused briefly when they reached a grassy plateau that gave them a spectacular view. The azure Pacific framed the scene below. Liz reached for her camera.

They rode for half an hour more. The forest was less dense now, and the ocean was often visible through the trees. Finally they turned toward the mountain, and in a few minutes reached their destination.

The clearing was a little Eden. A deep pool was filled by a waterfall almost thirty feet high, which spilled over a sheer face of rock. Mingled floral scents permeated the air; native ferns covered the ground and grew alongside the moss to the very edge of the pool. The soothing aura of green—every tint of green from emerald to jade—was punctuated by brilliant blossoms.

Her hands had gone limp on the pommel as she drank in the sight, spellbound. She couldn't help it; her eyes swam with tears. "How absolutely..." Beautiful was too tame a description. She didn't even think of her camera.

Justin cursed under his breath when he saw tears in those beautiful eyes. He wished they were here alone, wished he could take her in his arms and kiss away the tears.

Hell, he should have paid attention to his instincts and called early this morning to uninvite Babs and Jay. Then he and Liz could have had the day together. He hadn't done that because he had a feeling she would have used his maneuvering as an excuse not to take the trip at all.

Suddenly he was filled with an overwhelming urge to put his hands on her. He didn't even try to fight it. Swiftly he dismounted and reached up to catch her by the waist. Her eyes flew to his and she gripped his hard biceps. Her body slid down the length of him. He hadn't realized what effect the contact would have and he clenched his teeth against the sensation. When her feet reached the ground he dropped his hands instantly. "I'll see to the horses," he said gruffly. "You should put on your sweater; it's cooler at this altitude."

Liz shivered; surely this reaction was from the sudden drop in temperature and not his nearness. She'd thought he was exaggerating when he had cautioned that the glen would be shaded and chilly. "I didn't bring one," she admitted.

A tiny muscle jumped in his jaw. "You just can't take advice from me, can you?" he muttered.

As soon as the horses had been taken care of, he slung his saddlebags over his shoulder and joined the group. He'd managed to pull himself together. He should be accustomed to the sudden desire and the sudden irritation by now. "Lunch," he announced as he dropped the bags on a huge slab of rock. From one bag he took a sweater and tossed it to Liz.

She caught it reflexively. It was his. "Oh, I don't really—"

He silenced her with a look. "I don't know what we have but Annie has never disappointed us with a picnic," he said.

"Indeed she hasn't," said Babs, determinedly cheerful. "And I can't count the number of picnics we've had here, can you, Justin? Jay?"

Liz was fully aware of the intimacy shared by these three—Babs didn't have to make her question quite so pointed. She felt like an interloper anyway. She hurriedly pulled the sweater over her head. It smelled of him, clean and masculine.

Annie had lived up to her reputation. The food, at least, was a success. There was mouth-watering fried chicken, freshly baked rolls, crisp celery stuffed with a creamy cheese mixture and, for dessert, tea cakes flavored with mango and papaya. She had also included a thermos of hot coffee. They were quiet as they ate.

Finally Jay gave a huge sigh and stretched out on the carpet of ferns, his hands behind his head. "If I ate Annie's cooking every day I'd be as big as a house," he said.

They all laughed. Jay was thin as a rail.

Liz looked at him sympathetically. Poor Jay, she thought again. Poor Liz, her heart goaded.

He closed his eyes. "I'm going to take a nap. Wake me when it's time to leave."

Justin took his coffee cup and wandered over to sit on a rock next to the pool. Babs followed and they struck up a subdued conversation.

Liz didn't know what to do with herself so she began to pack the picnic things. She was startled when Jay spoke her name quietly. She looked at him. He had opened one eye. "Yes?" she answered.

"I'll survive."

She called up a smile. "Yes, I'm sure you will." She wished she were sure about herself.

When Babs came to help with the remains of lunch, Liz tensed.

"I have to talk to you," said the blonde.

Liz glanced at Jay; he was snoring softly. "I can't see that we have anything to discuss."

"What about this? Justin loves you."

Because he can't have you. Liz took a deep breath. "A relationship between us wouldn't work."

"Because of me?"

"What do you think?" Liz wasn't pleased by her own sharp tone but she simply couldn't help the way the words came out. She wished only that this woman would get away from her.

But Babs pressed on. "Look, I don't like you any more than you like me, but I'll let you in on a secret." She snapped a top onto a plastic bowl. "I've spent as much of my life around Fairwinds as I've spent at home. And from the time I was sixteen I was the one who chased Justin, not vice versa. We dated for a while, before his father died. He even thought about marrying me once, but our romance was like a bad habit. We both realized that it wasn't good for us, but we couldn't quite kick it." She tucked a foil-wrapped package into the saddlebag. "Luckily we realized that we weren't in tune before it was too late. We would have been miserable together."

"Why are you telling me all this?" Liz asked.

"Because I love Justin."

Liz didn't comment.

"He is my friend and I love him very much," Babs went on, her chin tilted. Then suddenly her entire body seemed to deflate. "I haven't done a lot of things in my life that I'm proud of. You were witness to one of the worst. But I am proud of being Justin Hogan's friend."

Liz sat speechless. Literally. No words formed in her brain or on her lips. Her thoughts were tumbling, though, presenting her with alternatives, options, potentialities. She fiddled with the tablecloth, folding it untidily, to give her hands something to do.

"I told him why you hated me," said Babs. "I told him about Taylor."

Shock, explosive and precipitate, put an immediate brake on Liz's thoughts, but freed her voice. "You *told* him?" Dear God, now Justin knew her greatest humiliation. She sat on her heels, staring dumbfounded at the other woman. Her eyes swung to Justin.

He was looking at her like—like he was sorry for her. Her first reaction was to flee, to run wildly, as fast and as far as possible. She cursed and flung the crumpled cloth away. She stood too suddenly, leaving the blood that was supposed to nourish her brain down in her feet. She felt light-headed, dizzy, and she staggered.

Babs's eyes widened at her reaction. Justin put down his coffee, made a move as though to stand. He looked worried.

Liz didn't care what either of them thought. Her needs were direct and simple—to get to the house, pack her bags and leave. She circled Jay's prone figure and stalked over to where the horses were tethered. As she released the chestnut mare, Justin came up behind her.

"Where do you think you're going?"

Anger was her foremost emotion right now, and she was grateful for the fortitude it gave her. She drew the reins over the mare's head and put her left foot in the stirrup. "I've had just about all I can take, Justin. I don't need your pity," she said furiously.

He held the horse's head in a firm grip. "Lady, pity is the last thing I'll ever feel for you," he said through clenched teeth. "What the hell did Babs say to you? I'll wring her neck. But you're not going anywhere until we all go."

Liz looked at him, at the harsh planes and worried lines in his face. Her anger dissolved. This excursion was meant to be a relaxing outing after days of hard work and nights with no sleep. Instead it had been a disastrous experience.

She longed, with every cell in her body, with every fragment of her being, to smooth the worried lines away, to comfort him, ease his pain. The prospect was heart-wrenching; he wasn't a man who wanted or needed comfort. "Justin, please, take me home," she murmured, crushed and distraught.

He must have read some of her feelings in her eyes, because a small smile played across his lips for a moment. He covered both her hands with one of his. "I'll get you home, honey," he told her in the low voice of reason. "But we all have to go together. Give me a minute to get the others organized, okay?"

She nodded. "Okay," she said softly.

They began their descent along the same trail they had taken this morning, but when they reached the plateau Babs called out, "Let's take the old trail. I'm tired and it's shorter."

"No way, Babs. I haven't checked the condition of that trail in months," said Justin.

"We're all experienced riders," she argued.

"I agree," said Liz. She wanted this trip to end and end quickly.

"I agree with Justin. If it's washed out, we'll have to turn back," warned Jay.

Babs tossed her blond head and started for a break in the trees. "Well, I'm going this way. I'll have a drink waiting for you when you get back to the house."

"Babs!" The command in Justin's voice halted her. "I'll lead," he said grimly.

Babs edged her horse in behind Justin's and Liz followed, leaving Jay to bring up the rear.

The trail was steeper but comfortably wide, following the edge of the mountain. The view was spectacular; from this height, the smoky color of deepening shadows from the mountains to the west blended with the sky to produce a vista that looked like a painting.

Liz could see, however, why Justin was wary of this route. There was a lot of loose rock and the horses were skittish. She kept a firm hand on Beth. They were almost three-quarters of the way down when the accident happened.

The trail doubled back on itself, and Liz had just passed the turn when all at once, from above her, Jay's horse dislodged some loose rock. Instinctively, she looked up. She realized instantly it was a fatal mistake.

She got a face full of dirt and dust. She closed her watering eyes, coughed and brushed at the debris. Beth began to dance nervously. It was impossible to see where she was going. She dismounted, speaking soothingly to the little mare as she went to her head to calm her.

But, blinded by the dust in her eyes, Liz didn't realize how close to the edge she was. Her foot dislodged more loose rock and she felt herself slipping. She had nothing to hold on to except the reins.

So she let go.

Her legs slid out from under her; she clawed desperately at the ledge, trying to find a handhold. There was nothing there; she kept sliding, more rock and debris sliding with her, pelting her face and shoulders. "Justin!" she screamed. "Justin!"

She heard him call her name, then a large stone hit her temple and she lost consciousness.

Chapter Eight

Liz slowly became aware of the unmatched security of Justin's strong arms crushing her to his broad chest, of his husky, broken voice calling to her. "Liz, oh, God, Liz. Please speak to me, baby."

"Justin."

"Yes, it's me," he told her unnecessarily. No other arms felt like his. "I've got you. You're all right."

She was reassured, too, by the sound of his heartbeat, pounding with runaway significance beneath her cheek. They weren't dead. She felt his lips, his warm breath on her face. But when he raised his head and brushed the hair away from her face, she panicked and gripped the front of his shirt. "Don't let go of me!"

Blindly his mouth sought hers and he kissed her with hunger and relief, and love. "Don't worry," he said, breaking off the kiss. Determination hardened his voice, but his touch was gentle on the spot where the rock had hit her. "I'm not going to let go." *Not ever. You are mine, Liz Ennis.* His silent declaration was a vow and a prayer of thanksgiving. He hung on to it as determinedly as she held on to him.

Jay's voice reached them. "Is she all right?" he called.

"Yes, she's okay," Justin answered.

Liz buried her face in his neck. "I was so scared." Her voice shook with nervous laughter; at the same time, she realized she was crying.

Justin's arms tightened and he laid his cheek against her head. When he spoke his voice shook. "So was I. God, I've never been so scared in my life."

He held her, simply held her, in that strong protective embrace. She reveled in the strength flowing from his body to hers. At last her head began to clear. She drew in a long breath and unclenched her fingers from the fabric of his shirt.

Justin felt her move and raised his head. She gave him a smile that was shaky but beautiful. "Where are we, by the way?" she asked.

Justin regained enough of his confidence to chuckle. "We're on a ledge about ten feet below the trail and we've got to figure a way to get up there," he said. "Can you see? Did you lose your contacts?"

Miraculously the contacts were still in place and her tears had washed them. "I can see."

Somehow they accomplished it. Liz was still shaking badly and she knew she was more a hindrance than a help. When they reached the ledge, Jay loosened the rope that Justin had tied firmly around her waist. "Thank God," he said. "You were almost killed."

Babs was white-faced and shaking almost as hard as Liz was. "I feel so guilty. If I hadn't insisted we take this trail..."

Liz touched her arm reassuringly. She was so glad to be alive that she was ready to love anybody, including Babs. "Please don't feel guilty. If you remember, I was the one who seconded your suggestion."

"Thanks," said Babs.

"Let's get home," said Justin.

Jay held out Beth's reins but Justin shook his head when Liz would have accepted them. "You can lead her horse, Jay. I'm taking her up with me."

Liz reached out to stroke Beth's velvety nose, but she was relieved. She was still groggy, her vision was a little blurred, and she wasn't sure her shaking hands were capable of control.

Justin mounted the black Arabian and bent to lift her in front of him. She relaxed against his broad chest as he gathered up the reins. He looked at her, muttered something and reached into his back pocket for a handkerchief. "You'd better hold this to your head until we get home."

She took the square of white linen from him and dabbed painfully at her temple. The handkerchief came away bloody. She managed a trembling laugh. "I must look like I've been in a fight."

"You look... beautiful." His mouth was warm against her head. "Rest if you can. We'll be home soon."

Home. The word had such a satisfying ring. Amazingly, she did rest. She was dozing when they reached the stables. Justin dismounted, tossed the reins to a hand and lifted Liz off King's back into his arms.

"I can walk, Justin," she murmured, still half asleep. "I'm fine."

Justin looked at her white face. "This is quicker," he growled as he headed for the house, ignoring the others.

Liz didn't argue with him. Despite her protest, she wasn't sure she could walk. Her senses spun alarmingly at every movement. She nestled her head against his shoulder and closed her eyes.

Sondra and Annie met them at the door with cries of alarm. Babs and Jay were right behind Justin, and they both began to explain. Justin cut them off. "Mother, call Dr. Pearson. Annie, come with me."

Liz roused herself. "I don't need a doctor," she protested forcefully. At least, she thought her protest was forceful.

Justin ignored her. "Tell him to hurry."

He mounted the steps quickly. Annie was there to open the bedroom door. As Justin started to lower Liz onto the white bedspread, she clutched at his neck. "Don't put me there, I'm filthy."

"I don't want to put you down at all. I don't want to take my arms away, not even for a minute. Do you understand why?"

His voice was low, meant for her ears only. Liz stared at him, the beginnings of a smile on her face.

Annie touched his arm. "A bath would make her feel better, Justin. I'll run a tub."

She felt as if she was wound as tight as a watch spring. "Please, Justin," said Liz. "Now that we're home I can stand."

Justin carefully set her feet on the floor but kept his arm around her. He looked down; for once his expression was completely open and unguarded. "Do you feel like you're at home, Liz?" he asked quietly.

Before she could answer Annie was back. "I'll take over from here, Justin."

Justin sighed impatiently and shot a look at Annie. He was tempted to tell her to get lost. But then he took another look at Liz. She was white and shaky. This wasn't the time to go into the problems surrounding their relationship. "I'll be back."

She looked at him. Her head throbbed too much right now to try to sort it all out but she was ready to acknowledge that something had changed between them, had been redefined and clarified. "Yes, please," she said, her eyes cloudy with the disorder of her thoughts. She watched his broad shoulders disappear through the doorway.

Liz unwound under Annie's soothing care. She had a quick bath, was helped into her gown and peignoir and tucked under the bedcovers. She relaxed and was ready to sleep the minute her head touched the pillow. "Thank you, Annie," she murmured. "You're very kind."

Annie gave that deprecating sniff that was so characteristic of her. "You're easy to be kind to, Liz."

Liz smiled and closed her eyes. Annie stood looking at her scratched and bruised face. In a few minutes, there was a knock on the door. The doctor came in followed by Justin and Sondra.

Justin's eyes narrowed at the vulnerable sight of Liz's white face against the white pillowcase. Vulnerability was so foreign to Liz Ennis, she wouldn't like being seen this way.

Sam Pearson was a rotund man with a fringe of white hair, and a lifelong friend of the Hogans. He had delivered Justin and, sadly, had pronounced his father dead. The look on Justin's face was one he'd never seen before. "Sondra, take Justin out of here," he ordered. "Annie is all the help I need."

When they were gone, the doctor turned to Liz. "Well, young lady, how does the other fellow look?"

"I'm afraid he got away without a scratch, Doctor," she answered, smiling with an effort.

"Let's have a look at you, then. Annie, would you close the blinds, please."

He poked and prodded, shone a tiny white light in her eyes, cleaned and bandaged the cut on her temple. After he finished his examination, he sat in the white wicker chair beside the bed and studied her for a moment, his finger on her pulse. At last he spoke. "You don't give much of yourself away, do you, Liz Ennis?"

She fought to keep her eyes open. "I don't understand, Doctor."

He smiled. "I know you're tired but I want to ask you a few more questions. Have you been under a particular amount of stress lately?"

Liz shifted her gaze away from his serious blue eyes. "Not really," she answered evasively.

He nodded. "Annie, you can tell the others that I'm finished." When she was gone he pressed for more. "The stress, now. Are you certain?"

She was struck by the effort it took for a simple smile. "No more than any other person who works for a living."

He thought for a minute. Then he sighed. "I should admit you to the hospital...."

That brought her fully awake. "No," she declared, struggling to rise.

He put his hand on her shoulder. "Well, if you'll promise—"

"I'll promise anything," she assured him. "I don't like hospitals."

The door opened and Justin and Sondra came in, followed by Annie. The energy it had taken to object had sapped her strength, and she fell back against the pillow. She fought to stay awake. She heard Sondra's voice as if from a distance. "How is she, Sam?"

"I can find no evidence of concussion. However, I am concerned by her drowsiness."

Liz gave up and closed her eyes. Their voices became a low hum.

An hour later she was deeply asleep when she heard Justin's deep voice calling her name. She struggled to rise from oblivion but it was no use.

His arm slipped beneath her shoulders and he lifted her. "Liz, wake up."

Why wouldn't he let her sleep? "Justin? What do you want?"

"Liz, open your eyes and look at me," he ordered in a stern voice.

Her lashes fluttered. The soft glow from the bedside lamp showed her the deep furrows of concern across his brow. "Why?" she complained. "I'm tired."

The hard planes of his face softened into a smile. "I know, honey, I know you're tired. You can go back to sleep now."

Again, later, he called to her, lifted her, made her look at him and speak. She answered with a sob. "Justin Hogan, I knew you were a hard man but I didn't know you were cruel."

Gently he laid her back on the pillow and smoothed her hair. She felt his lips on her eyelids before she descended again into a sound sleep.

The next time he roused her, she was angry, then pleading, then resigned. It seemed that every time she roused herself enough to protest he withdrew.

* * *

Liz opened her eyes. She was surprised to see Justin sitting in the white wicker chair next to her bed. What . . . ? He was leaning forward, his elbows on his knees, his forehead resting on clasped fingers. His face was hidden from her but his dark hair was tangled as though he'd repeatedly and impatiently run his fingers through it.

She frowned, trying to remember why Justin was in her room, then it all came back in a rush of emotion that was part horror, part relief. She reached out to smooth his mussed hair.

His head came up suddenly and he gripped her hand tightly between both of his. His eyes blazed with an emotion she couldn't put a name to, then their color was lost to her as his lids fell. He lifted her hand to his mouth and kissed her palm. She hadn't been aware of the tension radiating from his broad shoulders until it began to dissipate.

At last he raised his head again and gave her a half smile as he intertwined her fingers with his. He spoke softly into the silent comfort of the room. "How do you feel?" he asked.

Liz touched the bandage at her temple with her free hand—not for anything would she have withdrawn the one he held—and returned his smile. "Not too bad, considering I'm holding hands with the thief who keeps robbing me of my sleep."

A corner of his mouth tilted up a degree. "Sorry," he murmured unapologetically. "But you, my beautiful grouch, are a terrible patient."

There was something so pleasant about being alone with him in a dark, quiet house in the middle of the night. "Terrible? Why? What's wrong with me?"

He hesitated a moment before he answered. "Probably nothing, thank God, but the doctor wanted to be sure there was no concussion. You have to be wakened every hour or so until morning."

"And you volunteered for the duty? What time is it now?"

Without releasing her hand, he glanced at his watch. "One-fifteen."

"Justin, you must be exhausted," she murmured.

"You don't think I'd trust this job to anyone else, do you? You'd have them talked into letting you swim laps in the pool."

"I can't put one over on you, can I?"

"Not a chance. Are you hungry? Annie brought up some soup in the thermos."

Her mouth felt as if she had the whole Sahara Desert in there. She started to shake her head, but the first twinge of pain reminded her that it wouldn't be such a good idea. She said instead, "No, but I could use something cold to drink."

He still held on to her hand. "There's juice and water."

She opted for the juice. He seemed reluctant to release her, but he poured the juice and lifted her carefully, with an arm behind her shoulders, for her to sip from the glass.

"Thanks," she said when she was finished. The effort had taken something out of her and she felt her lids grow heavy again. She fought it; Justin had never seemed so caring, so accessible.

But she was losing the battle. "I think I'm going to have to say...good-night...again." As she drifted away, she felt his lips in her hair. They felt wonderful; she didn't know when she was awake or dreaming.

Justin could not look away. He wanted to absorb every expression on her face, to make her a part of him, store enough memories to console him through the long weeks, months, years ahead.

Sitting here watching her through the hours, he'd realized finally that Liz Ennis could never be his. He wasn't sure she could ever belong to any man and he berated himself for his autocratic treatment of her. She had feelings for him; she might even think they were love.

But if he tried to capitalize on those feelings, if he used them to keep her here, he would eventually kill the thing he loved most about her—her bright, independent spirit.

And he could not walk away from his responsibilities to his family, his employees. He loved the ranch, was proud of the traditions established by his father. He'd never given a thought to spending his life here. Until Liz came along.

Now, for the first time he resented the hell out of those responsibilities. He'd never questioned them before. He'd simply accepted that the ranch was a part of his life, of what he was. He had no choice.

Neither did she. She would never be happy here— oh, maybe for a while she would. But the wanderlust would return. She would grow to resent him, to hate him. He would rather be alone than have that happen.

It was agonizing to think of her leaving for even a day; at this moment, he couldn't dwell on thoughts of her being lost to him forever.

It was almost four when Liz once more opened her eyes spontaneously. Justin's head was resting against the back of the chair, which had been shifted slightly so that he was facing her. He was relaxed, breathing evenly, possibly sleeping. His long legs were crossed at the ankles, stretched out. But he still held her hand.

She glanced beyond him toward the window. A lifting of the dark, rather than definite light, indicated that the long night would soon be over.

Her gaze returned to him. Her lips formed a smile. All the love that had been growing within her heart since she arrived at Fairwinds shimmered in her eyes. She was filled with contentment and a yearning such as she had never known. She knew now that her life, her career, meant nothing when weighed against her love for this extraordinary man.

Justin opened his eyes and looked at her. Neither of them could look away, neither could break the visual bond. Neither wished to. Everything in the room receded, as though there were only the two of them in the whole world, joined by their clasped hands and the love in their locked gazes.

Liz swallowed over the obstruction in her throat. "I never did get to use my last wish," she whispered cautiously.

He didn't smile. "No, you didn't."

"I wish I could feel your arms around me."

With a groan Justin came out of the chair and onto the bed, pulling her none too gently off the pillow and into his arms.

Liz grinned at him. "That didn't hurt a bit," she teased.

When he would have gentled toward her she wouldn't let him. She wound her arms around his neck and raised her parted lips. The kiss, initiated by her, instantly became his show. He angled his mouth over hers and thrust with his tongue. She combed his dark hair with her fingers, ran her restless hands over his broad shoulders, tried to mold herself more closely to his chest. At last, she could feel the beat of his heart, exactly in rhythm with hers, against her breasts.

"I love you." Did she say that? Or was it Justin? It didn't matter.

Finally they both needed to breathe and Liz felt the shudder that went through him as he reluctantly tore his lips from hers. "Oh, God, Liz, if anything had happened to you—" His mouth crushed hers again, hungrily, devouring, as though a taste of her would never be enough.

In the tempest of emotion that enveloped her, all her misgivings disappeared as though swept away by a benevolent wind. Her heart soared. Justin loved her; she knew now that she was his first, his only choice. He loved her as much as she loved him. It wouldn't be easy, but with love on their side, they could blend their lives. Surely they could.

"Why don't you lie here beside me?" she murmured against his lips.

He eased himself down on the bed. She squirmed a bit, making room for him, then she nestled against his hard shoulder. "Isn't that better?"

"Annie will kill me if she catches me in your bed."

Liz chuckled. "Then you'd have to make an honest woman of me. I wouldn't mind that."

When he didn't answer she tilted her head back to look at him. His green eyes were black with an emotion that looked almost like pain. As she watched, his pupils contracted and his heavily lashed lids came down to screen his expression.

Disquieted, she raised her head and touched his cheek. "Justin? You did ask me to marry you?"

"Liz." He tangled his fingers in her silky hair and gave her a tender kiss. "Babe, we have a lot to think about, but not tonight." He guided her head gently, unerringly to the place on his shoulder where she was most comfortable. "Go to sleep," he ordered gruffly, and deliberately closed his eyes.

She watched him for a minute more, but his eyelids didn't flicker. She set aside her disquiet and closed her eyes. He was right. They did have a lot to think about, but her brain was too tired.

The next time Liz woke she was cold and bereft. The bed next to her was empty. Annie rocked in a chair across a room flooded with sunlight. Had she dreamed the whole long night?

Annie saw that she was awake. She set aside her mending and came to the bed. "Well, you look much better. Can I fix you some breakfast? The doctor will be here soon."

Liz was disoriented. "Just coffee, please, Annie."

"You need a little something in your stomach. I'll bring you a piece of toast." Annie turned toward the door.

Liz rose onto one elbow. "Did I—Justin . . . was he here?"

"Indeed he was," answered Annie. "All night long. But he left an hour ago."

Liz was stunned. "Left?" she said unsteadily.

"On a plane for Dallas. You remember the business trip to Texas, don't you? He was scheduled to leave the day after the cows got sick. He put it off as long as he could but the folks in Texas were getting anxious and he was afraid they'd sell that prize bull he wanted to someone else if he delayed any longer."

Of course, now she remembered. But could one more hour matter so much that he couldn't wait to say goodbye? He hadn't asked her to wait for him. He hadn't told her that he loved her.

"I'll be right back with that coffee and some toast, too." Annie left.

Liz couldn't believe the terrible weight that had suddenly taken up residence inside her chest. Tears welled in her eyes as she lay back, and she let them come. The night was such a blur, her recall so confusing; but Justin had held her in his arms. He *had* told her he loved her, hadn't he? Or had she imagined it?

Justin stared blindly at the sapphire blue ocean below him. He had a long flight ahead and he should be working on the papers he'd stuffed into his briefcase at the last minute. Since the crisis on the ranch it was imperative that he get this bull to add new blood to the herd. And it was a perfect excuse to get away from Fairwinds.

Maybe by the time he returned she would be gone, finished with her assignment, out of his life.

But never out of his heart, a voice inside reminded.

The flight attendant came to take his order for breakfast. She was young and blonde and beautiful, but he couldn't summon one shred of enthusiasm for her agreeable smile.

It would be easier this way, he told himself again and again. Hell, he'd been telling himself that from the minute he left her room this morning.

Muttering a string of curses, he reached under the seat in front of him for his briefcase. He pulled down the tray and got to work.

After two days, Liz had been pronounced cured. She could no longer delay the work she had to do. She called the hotel where she had made reservations and explained why she hadn't arrived when she was expected. Yes, they could take her, they said. Two days on the Kona Coast would do it for this assignment. By then Justin would be home.

Sondra and Annie were encouraging her to return to Fairwinds when she'd finished in Kona, and she'd agreed. She was going to wait for Justin, whether he wanted her to wait or not. She was going to insist that they talk this over. He couldn't leave her hanging.

He had called twice, but neither time had he asked to speak to her. That had hurt, cut deeply. She couldn't conceive of why, but she intended to have an answer before she left Hawaii.

A week later, Liz decided that she should have saved that last wish. She had finally accepted what was staring her in the face. Justin was deliberately prolonging his trip. And she was still asking herself the same question—why? Her confidence was ebbing quickly.

She'd finished her work on the other side of the island and returned to the ranch. She'd made a turn-around trip to Honolulu, to Fran Mason's office, to deliver the transparencies, and she'd been waiting since. But it was stupid to think she could remain at Fairwinds much longer.

The phone call, when it came, was almost a relief. Annie called her in from outside, where she'd been watching one of the men exercise Beth. The line from New York was so clear the editor could have been in the next room. A representative from the magazine was passing through Honolulu tomorrow, she was told, and would like to meet with her to discuss the assignment in India.

Liz raked her fingers through her hair and sighed as she sank into a chair. Justin was making excuses not to return while she was still at Fairwinds. His message could not be clearer.

She had no valid reason for refusing, so she arranged to meet the man for dinner the next night and called her parents.

Sondra and Annie walked her to her car. Sondra had heatedly protested her leaving. Annie was quiet, but her obvious disappointment consoled Liz, as well. But their emotions were nothing compared to her devastation at having to go. As she lifted the heavy camera case into the car, she said, "Tell Justin—" She paused and looked at his home. "Never mind," she said.

Chapter Nine

The sun had reached its zenith. It beat down mercilessly on Justin's head. He was in a lousy mood. A really lousy mood. He kept his left hand on the reins while he took off his Stetson with his right and wiped his damp brow with his forearm.

King danced and he brought the horse under control with the pressure of his knees. "Don't you start acting up on me, too," he grumbled.

He had come home yesterday, feeling—and looking—like a wrung-out sweatband. His mother had greeted him with restraint, her disapproval evident.

At breakfast this morning she had started in. "I just don't understand why you had to leave without even saying goodbye to Liz," she'd said. "The poor girl was very upset."

Justin had explained before he left how important this trip was to the business of running this place.

"Hell, this isn't the Parker ranch, Mother," he told her, mentioning the huge spread nearby that was the largest privately owned ranch in the United States. "We've just lost forty-seven damned cows."

Sondra's expression had tightened. "You don't have to lecture to me, Justin. *Or* use offensive language. I am perfectly aware how dangerous the virus was, but don't try to suggest the ranch is in danger of failing. With your breeding operation, we could lose all the cows tomorrow and not go bankrupt."

Justin had sighed. "Mother, she wouldn't be happy here," he said, going directly to the root of the discussion.

"So you do care for her?"

His gaze had fallen under the delight in hers. "Mother—"

"I knew it! I knew you were perfect the minute I saw you together. And don't tell me you don't love her. It's as plain as the nose on your face."

"Mother, let me ask you something."

"Of course, dear."

"What are the things you like most about Liz?"

Sondra had clearly been bewildered by the question. "What do you mean?"

Justin picked up a spoon and stirred the coffee in his cup, despite the fact that it contained neither sugar nor cream. He'd been through all this in his mind—many times—and he gave her the answer he'd come up with to fight his own loneliness. "Let me see if I can answer the question for you, then. Liz is bright and beautiful. She's developed her own independence and is a very successful photographer. Do you think she would be content to settle down to the life-style that is necessary for me? Give up her traveling? And what if she did? You've told me more than once that marriage isn't all romance. What would happen five years down the road, when the gloss has worn off, when she started to get restless?" He sighed deeply. "Don't you see, Mother?" Even though he knew it was impossible, the subject was enough to bring back a spark of hope, of "maybe, if," of "could it work?" The recurring pain he felt was unbearable. "I've been burned once. I don't intend to chance it again."

She picked up on it, just as he'd known she would. "But you never really loved her." Sondra dismissed Babs with a wave of her hand. Then she hesitated. "That was us, the parents," she added more thoughtfully. "But you do love Liz."

"Exactly. What if I *had* loved Babs? What if I'd been devastated when she married someone else? Wouldn't you have felt guilty for trying to arrange our lives?"

"Yes, but, Justin—"

He ended the discussion once and for all, interrupting in a low, dangerous voice. "Mother," he said. "Butt out." He dropped the spoon on the saucer with a clunk, scraped his chair back from the table and left the room through the back door. Fast.

His mother didn't have a comeback for his last remark.

The car pulled to the curb and stopped. Liz reached over the seat and hugged her father, who was at the wheel of the car, then her mother. "You take care of each other. I'll write as soon as I get to New Delhi to let you know where I'll be staying."

Betsy twisted around to look worriedly at her daughter. "We'll miss you, darling. I wish you'd let us walk you to the gate," she said, raising her voice to be heard over the sound of airport noise.

"I'm cutting it close as it is. By the time you parked the car the plane would be in the air."

Liz was looking directly into the afternoon sun. Its brilliance made her eyes water, and she blinked. In a lifetime of goodbyes, this leave-taking was suddenly the most difficult she'd ever experienced—worse, much worse than a year ago. She had no misconceptions about why. Justin. Her heart felt so heavy in her chest that it was hard to breathe. For a wild moment, she wished she were ten again and content to let these two people she loved make her decisions for her.

Her father seemed to read her thoughts. He gripped her hand in a comforting squeeze. "Do you have enough money?" he said quietly. The admiral never had to raise his voice to be heard, not even over the thrust of a jet engine.

With an effort, she smiled and nodded. She released her hand gently, made herself open the back door and climbed out. "Bye, Daddy. Bye, Mother."

Quickly, she grabbed her camera case and shut the door behind her. Her mother pressed the trunk release from inside. Liz hauled her small duffel bag out and hooked the strap over her shoulder. More than one head turned to watch the tall, confident redhead, dressed in khaki walking shorts and a bush jacket, weighted down with odd-looking bags. Giving her parents a last wave, she entered the terminal building.

At last, she was alone. Not literally alone, of course, but anonymous in the crowd. She didn't have to struggle to keep a composed expression on her face any longer. If she wanted to cry, she could cry without being concerned who saw her.

Not that she wanted to cry. In fact she was angry with herself when she realized that she indeed had tears seeping from her eyes.

She coughed out a laugh that sounded like a sob as she recalled that first night in Justin's study at Fairwinds. He had admonished her not to cry another tear for Taylor; the damned fool wasn't worth it, he'd said.

Justin hadn't mentioned crying for himself. She wouldn't be feeling this miserable if he'd just said goodbye . . . if he'd just told her he'd miss her . . .

As she strode toward the international gate, she dug into her case for her ticket and passport and a handful of tissues. Tears didn't solve a thing, she told herself firmly. She was through with them.

Her long legs ate up the distance and soon she found herself in the security line behind two sailors and a family of four.

The line moved slowly and she began to wonder if she would make her flight after all. Her duffel would go through the X ray but her camera cases would have to be searched by hand. She glanced at her watch and relaxed. She'd make it with time to spare.

That night Justin sat at his desk nursing a drink. It was his third, but unfortunately he was still cold sober. The Scotch hadn't helped dull the pain. Sober as a judge, he thought with disgust. The single desk lamp threw a puddle of light over the papers in front of him but he'd been ignoring them for the last hour.

The loneliness was almost tangible—like a weight on his chest. Damn it, this was his house, but she seemed to have taken it over. In the dining room the chandelier reflected highlights in her auburn hair; in the empty kitchen he could hear her voice as she chattered with Annie. He looked across the study at the leather-covered sofa and saw her curled up there, her feet tucked under her, listening to him talk about things she should see on the island. In the stables he could see her on Beth's back, and that brought the memory of her near-fatal accident to his mind.

That image was the most destructive. Her white face. The blood at her temple.

He shuddered and ground his teeth—he couldn't deal with that at all, couldn't handle it. He put a hand to his eyes, blocking the light for a minute, and reached for the Scotch bottle with the other.

A slight noise, like a whisper, a current of motion from the doorway, stayed his hand. He looked up. His eyes fixed on a shadow beyond the pool of light; he didn't—couldn't—move; he didn't even breathe, for endless seconds.

Then, with a groan like the cry of a wounded animal, he dropped his hand and spun the swivel chair around to face the blank wall behind him. An expletive burst from his lips. "Damn it, now I'm seeing things!" he declared.

"No, you're not," Liz said to the broad shoulders. "But it's very encouraging that you think so."

He whirled back and stared at her for an endless minute. Then he was on his feet, circling the desk. She raised her head, ready for his kiss, ready to go into his arms.

But Justin clamped down hard on her shoulders instead, holding her at arm's length. "What the hell are you doing here? You're supposed to be in India."

Liz could feel the electricity surging from his hands into her shoulders and throughout her body. He might pretend to be angry—or unaffected—but there was no mistaking that it was only pretense. His eyes told another story completely.

Her lips curved into a small smile and she looked around as though she was surprised to find herself here. "Mmm. I am, aren't I? Looks like I missed the plane."

He gave her a little shake and said coldly, "Don't be a smart a—leck."

His gaze roved over her with a hunger that caught at her heart and weakened her legs, but his expression didn't thaw. A trace of misgiving, lasting no longer than the flicker of an eyelash, caused her smile to falter. She fought it back; she couldn't be wrong, she couldn't. He loved her. She was as certain of that as she was of her own feelings. He loved her enough to work through the problems that their relationship would cause.

Deliberately, she laid her hand on his chest. "I'm really pleased to hear that you're trying to clean up your language, Justin. It will be so much easier now than waiting until the children come."

Suddenly, to her utter delight, she was hauled into his arms, crushed against his broad chest. She wrapped her arms around his waist and clung to him. She felt his breath against her neck. He was calling her a silly fool, but she didn't take offense because the words were just words, and they were uttered in the most loving, broken voice.

Justin had suffered deeply, too. The realization brought tears to her eyes.

"Justin. It's over," she said softly. "It's all over. I love you, my heart, and I'm going to stay here and prove it to you. Somehow we'll work it out."

His eyes were moist when he raised his head and looked at her. Finally, at last, when she thought she couldn't stand it any longer, he kissed her.

It was quite a while before either of them spoke. He slid his hand from under her khaki shirt. "Are you sure you want to marry me, Liz?"

She rolled her eyes.

"If we marry, babe, it will be forever. I'll try not to tie you down, I want you to go on with your career, and I'll travel with you whenever I can, but the responsibility for the ranch is still mine. I can't walk away from it."

She touched his face. "My career is important to me, I won't deny that. But not as important as you are. Before I met you, I think I was afraid to slow my pace for long enough to think about what I really wanted.

"When you left—" She was glad she could laugh about that terrible day. "Honestly, Justin, I hate long drawn-out goodbyes, but that was ridiculous."

"I had to leave quickly," he said seriously, disregarding her attempt to lighten the moment. His hand moved restlessly on her arm. "I couldn't stay, Liz. I was feeling so damned possessive after your accident, I was afraid I would tie you to my side and you'd grow to hate me."

She had started shaking her head before he finished. "I could never hate you, my love," she murmured.

This kiss began gently, like a vow, but the sudden heat generated by the meeting of their lips wouldn't be denied and it became very hungry, very quickly.

Later as she sat within his arms on the leather sofa, she spoke again. "I really do have to go to India, you know. I promised."

"I know," said Justin, his fingers playing with a strand of flame-colored hair. "How long will you have to be there?"

"That depends. Do I go before or after our wedding?" she asked.

Justin thought for a moment. "Hell, I guess you'd better go before," he said disgustedly. "Once I have you in my bed, I intend to keep you there, for a while at least. How long will it take to finish the assignment?"

"Two weeks?"

"Are you asking me? Before you walked in this room tonight, I'd already decided to come after you, all the way to India, if necessary."

"Really?" She put her hand on his rough cheek. "I'll never know, will I?"

He laughed. "Call your editor tomorrow. And then call the Air India counter in Honolulu. I was mad as hell, too, that I hadn't caught you before the plane took off."

Justin rolled to his side, propping himself on one elbow to look at his wife. His other hand began moving over her sun-warmed skin. "Let's go swimming," he murmured into her ear. His lips found the sensitive spot on her neck.

Liz smiled, her eyes closed. Over the past seven days she had discovered—with the help of her husband—depths of sensuality in herself that amazed her. Justin's lovemaking had shown her what her body was made for.

Lifting herself on her elbows, she opened her eyes to look out over the calm lagoon. "That sounds good." She got to her feet, brushed off the sand and began to walk slowly toward the water.

Mesmerized for a minute at the sight of her beautiful body outlined by the dying sun's golden rays, Justin thought with satisfaction how much he loved calling this magnificent woman, "wife." He linked his hands behind his head and lay back on the sand.

Life with Liz would never be dull. He smiled. She had given him hell when she found out about this private beach house. She'd actually made him promise to buy new furniture for it while she was in India. She wouldn't sleep with him on a bed where any other woman had slept. "Not that I imagine you did much sleeping," she snapped.

She wasn't gone quite two weeks but the furniture was in place when she got home.

Liz turned to look at him. "Are you coming?" she called.

"What do you think," he growled, rolling over. He jackknifed to his feet and caught her on the run.

* * * * *

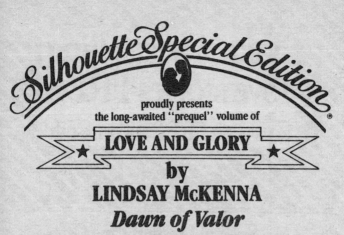

Silhouette Special Edition

proudly presents
the long-awaited "prequel" volume of

★ LOVE AND GLORY ★

by
LINDSAY McKENNA
Dawn of Valor

In the summer of '89, Silhouette Special Edition premiered three novels
celebrating America's men and women in uniform: LOVE AND GLORY,
by bestselling author Lindsay McKenna. Featured were the proud
Trayherns, a military family as bold and patriotic as the American
flag—three siblings valiantly battling the threat of dishonor, determined
to triumph . . . in love and glory.

Now, discover the roots of the Trayhern brand of courage, as parents
Chase and Rachel relive their earliest heartstopping experiences of
survival and indomitable love, in

Dawn of Valor, Silhouette Special Edition #649

This month, experience the thrill of LOVE AND GLORY—from the very
beginning!

Take 4 bestselling love stories FREE

Plus get a FREE surprise gift!

Special Limited-time Offer

Mail to   **Silhouette Reader Service®**

In the U.S.   In Canada
3010 Walden Avenue   P.O. Box 609
P.O. Box 1867   Fort Erie, Ontario
Buffalo, N.Y. 14269-1867   L2A 5X3

YES! Please send me 4 free Silhouette Romance® novels and my free surprise gift. Then send me 6 brand-new novels every month, which I will receive months before they appear in bookstores. Bill me at the low price of $2.25* each. There are no shipping, handling or other hidden costs. I understand that accepting the books and gift places me under no obligation ever to buy any books. I can always return a shipment and cancel at any time. Even if I never buy another book from Silhouette, the 4 free books and the surprise gift are mine to keep forever.

*Offer slightly different in Canada—$2.25 per book plus 69¢ per shipment for delivery.

Sales tax applicable in N.Y. Canadian residents add applicable federal and provincial sales tax.

215 BPA HAYY (US)   315 BPA 8176 (CAN)

Name _____ (PLEASE PRINT)

Address _____ Apt. No. _____

City _____ State/Prov. _____ Zip/Postal Code _____

This offer is limited to one order per household and not valid to present Silhouette Romance® subscribers. Terms and prices are subject to change.

SROM-BPADR   © 1990 Harlequin Enterprises Limited

SILHOUETTE·INTIMATE·MOMENTS®

NORA ROBERTS
Night Shadow

People all over the city of Urbana were asking, Who was that masked man?

Assistant district attorney Deborah O'Roarke was the first to learn his secret identity . . . and her life would never be the same.

The stories of the lives and loves of the O'Roarke sisters began in January 1991 with NIGHT SHIFT, Silhouette Intimate Moments #365. And if you want to know more about Deborah and the man behind the mask, look for NIGHT SHADOW, Silhouette Intimate Moments #373, available in March at your favorite retail outlet.

NITE-1

Silhouette Books®